THE CODYS OF WYOMING

```
                    Mark Cody        m.        Catherine Alder
                    (1870–1925)                (1880–1960)

        Walker Cody                        James Cody
        (1905–1976)                        (b. 1902; lost in WWII)

Joanne Baum      m.      Walker Cody

(1913–1983)

                 John Walker                         Anne Keller
                 (b. 1940)                           (b. 1950)

Mark James
(b. 1936 ran away in 1950)

                                    m.

        James (Jesse) Cody    Walker Cody    Dexter (Dex) Cody    Dusty Cody    Ellen Cody
        (b. 1975)             (b. 1977)      (b. 1979)            (b. 1979)     (b. 1982)
                                             Twin to Dusty        Twin to Dex

Mark Hansen
(b. 1974)
```

Dear Reader,

There's nothing more fun or more challenging than getting the whole family together to plan a big fiftieth wedding anniversary party or a huge family reunion. It takes many minds to think of the hundreds of details and make it all come off without a hitch. Would it interest you to know that getting a group of authors together to plan a continuity isn't any different?

Imagine my excitement when I was asked to write the first of six books in the new continuity for Harlequin American Romance called THE CODYS: THE FIRST FAMILY OF RODEO. Woo hoo! Just the word *rodeo* sent a thrill through me. Within a few minutes of that phone call my mind was conjuring up a picture of my brooding hero, Walker. He's a former bulldogging champion and wounded war vet whose reunion with his outstanding rodeo family, after years of being away, brings joy and pain.

Pretty soon the other authors received their calls and before long the e-mails were flying back and forth as we proceeded to create a living, breathing, premier rodeo family living in the Buffalo Bill country of Cody, Wyoming, the most exciting area of the American West. The logistics of dates, times, people, events, family history, intrigue, romance, not to mention the blueprint for the layout of the six-hundred-thousand-acre Cottonwood Ranch, boggled the mind, but we did it!

Here's hoping we've provided a feast that will bring you thrills, chills and hours of reading pleasure.

Enjoy!

Rebecca Winters

Walker: The Rodeo Legend
REBECCA WINTERS

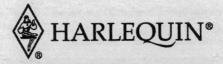

HARLEQUIN®

TORONTO • NEW YORK • LONDON
AMSTERDAM • PARIS • SYDNEY • HAMBURG
STOCKHOLM • ATHENS • TOKYO • MILAN • MADRID
PRAGUE • WARSAW • BUDAPEST • AUCKLAND

Recycling programs
for this product may
not exist in your area.

ISBN-13: 978-0-373-75314-7

WALKER: THE RODEO LEGEND

This edition published by arrangement with Harlequin Books S.A.

For questions and comments about the quality of this book
please contact us at Customer_eCare@Harlequin.ca

® and TM are trademarks of the publisher. Trademarks indicated with
® are registered in the United States Patent and Trademark Office, the
Canadian Trade Marks Office and in other countries.

www.eHarlequin.com

Printed in U.S.A.

ABOUT THE AUTHOR

Rebecca Winters, whose family of four children has now swelled to include five beautiful grandchildren, lives in Salt Lake City, Utah, in the land of the Rocky Mountains. With canyons and high alpine meadows full of wildflowers, she never runs out of places to explore. They, plus her favorite vacation spots in Europe, often end up as backgrounds for her romance novels, because writing is her passion, along with her family and church. Rebecca loves to hear from readers. If you wish to e-mail her, please visit her Web site at www.cleanromances.com.

Books by Rebecca Winters

To my old friend Jeff Butler from our Lausanne, Suisse, days who's a bulldogger extraordinare. *Merci mille fois* for your knowledge and insights. You helped me bring Walker Cody to life.

To Greg Wolfley, a wonderful landscape architect who helped me design the exciting career for Paula Olsen, *the* woman in Walker's life.

Chapter One

May 1

"Clay!" Paula Olsen screamed in horror. One second her little blond two-year-old had tumbled headfirst out of the Red Flyer wagon onto the asphalt. In the next second, a stranger plucked him away as a snarling black Lab in the town's Dog-Walkathon lunged forward to sink his teeth into her little boy.

It was all over in an instant. The man more or less thrust Clay into her arms, giving her a glimpse of darkly lashed green eyes. She looked her son over. Except for a red bump on his head from the fall, she didn't see a mark on him. "How can I ever thank you?" she called out to the man.

But he'd disappeared without saying anything, making it impossible for her to thank him properly. It was no use calling him back. He moved like the wind and was already gone.

She heard a male voice in the crowd say, "Ooh-eee! I believe that was J. W. Cody's son! I thought he was still overseas!"

Two and a half years ago a pregnant Paula had done the master plan for the landscaping of John Walker Cody's spectacular new ranch house, the latest addition to the famed Cottonwood Ranch built on their 600,000 acre spread outside Markton, Wyoming. The fabulously wealthy Codys were the premier family of rodeo in the northwestern part of the state. She was aware he had a daughter and four sons, all rodeo champions, but she'd never met any of them.

If her recollection was correct, one of them was an officer in the Marines. Could that be Clay's rescuer? If so, he was out of uniform.

He'd been tall, maybe six foot two or three and in his late twenties, but she only caught a brief view of chiseled male features. For some strange reason she couldn't get rid of the fleeting impression that he'd looked…haunted, and not just because of the incident.

"Oh, Paula—" her friend Angie Gregson spoke behind her, holding Danice. She'd been pulling her two-year-old in a wagon right in front of Paula. "Talk about a close call!"

"It was," Paula whispered in a shaken voice, hugging Clay tighter. The man had a familiar build and midnight-black hair, like J. W. Cody, so she figured the stranger had to be a Cody. While everyone else stood there frozen, only someone with his quick instincts and skill could have pulled Clay away from those gaping jaws in time.

"Listen, Angie… I'm going to take Clay to the car and get the stroller. Without a restraint, the wagon's just too dangerous." The thought of what would have happened without the stranger's masterful intervention refused to leave her mind.

"I'll go with you. Some of the big dogs are scaring Danice anyway."

Paula nodded. "I'm pretty sure it was that huge black Lab that frightened Clay, but when he fell out of the wagon, he ended up scaring the dog." Together they pulled the empty wagons down the sidewalk and around the corner to Paula's car.

For the families living in Markton, Wyoming, a town of 997 people, the First of May was a big deal. The annual dog parade drew people from all the surrounding communities, including nearby Cody where she and Angie lived in the same apartment complex.

The two of them had made a special trip over here for the fundraising event showing off people's own dogs as well as those from the Humane Society. Paula wished she could laugh about it, but the close call—even though all the dogs were on leash—could have sent Clay to the hospital to be stitched up. After losing her husband, Brent, in the war in Afghanistan eighteen months ago, she couldn't fathom anything serious happening to Clay.

"Are you all right?" her brunette friend asked after they'd loaded their toddlers in the strollers.

"I will be in a minute." If that man was a Cody, she knew where to find him and thank him.

An intuitive Angie touched her arm. "If you want to go home, we can."

"Don't be silly." After eighteen months of grieving for Brent, she would have thought she was getting past the worst of it, but for some reason this incident brought her emotions to the surface once more. "We've been looking forward to this." She wasn't about to let what happened ruin their plans. "It's getting warmer out. Let's drop in the ice-cream store on our way back to the dog parade."

"And then let's walk around Old Trail Town. I'm craving one of those Wild Bill Cody chili dogs."

"Sounds good to me." Maybe the walk would bring back Paula's appetite.

MOMENTS AGO WALKER CODY had left the motel on foot only to run into a dog parade, of all things. To see so many animals at once brought out children's excited cries and laughter from the adults, but Walker's attention had been captured by a blond toddler in a little wagon who was frightened by them. It reminded him of his own fear of horses as a child.

He noticed the boy start to stand up, then topple out, drawing the big Lab's attention. When it growled and bared its teeth, a woman's terrified cry followed. It was the kind he'd been trying to block from his subconscious since leaving Iraq.

Acting on pure instinct, Walker had torn through the line of onlookers and swooped the boy away before the person holding the leash could get control of the dog. But to his horror the incident brought on one of his flashbacks. While hugging the wailing child to his body, pressing him against his plastic-surgery scars, he'd broken out in a cold sweat.

Get away, Cody! Don't hurt anyone. Please, God, don't let me hurt anyone.

Blindly he handed off the child to the frightened woman standing next to him. Among the cacophony of sounds coming from the dogs and the crowd, Walker took off on a run. The last image in his mind had been of a pair of hot blue eyes turning to him in gratitude.

Her words had been spoken in English, not Arabic, which only added to his confusion and stayed with him all the way down the next block, where he found a bolt hole. Once in the men's bathroom at the Spotted Horse Saloon, he vomited.

Nothing came up but bile. He hadn't had an appetite since he'd flown home from Bethesda Naval Hospital three days ago. While he'd escaped the full blast of an IED, his two best buddies had taken the brunt. They would never get the chance to come home and live in a walking nightmare.

Post-traumatic stress disorder. That's what every guy in his outfit thought about, whether they admitted it or not. It was what they dreaded *if* their maimed bodies made it back. He'd had three episodes in the hospital where he'd been for the past two months, but this flashback had come when he couldn't pull out the dime he kept in his pocket.

He reached for it now and pressed it in the palm of his

hand. His counselor at the hospital told him, "When you feel unreal, disoriented, 'crazy,' like you can feel your mind slipping away, hold that dime in your hand very tightly and say to yourself, 'I am not crazy. I am not in Iraq. This isn't really happening now. I am safe now,' over and over again. Be very sure you tell yourself, 'I am safe now. I am not in Iraq.' The feeling of safety is crucial during the flashbacks.

"Also tell yourself, 'I am not going to hurt anyone.' Many returning vets suffering flashbacks are afraid they're going crazy and they'll hurt people. They're not crazy, but the danger to yourself is real, because sometimes you might try to rationalize the situation by believing that it's better to hurt yourself than to hurt anyone else. You need that spoken reinforcement to help you regain your feeling of being in control of yourself."

Walker reached in his pocket and pressed the dime into his palm, repeating the words like a litany. He was no longer aware of time or place. When he eventually became cognizant of his surroundings, he staggered over to the sink. No sooner had he rinsed out his mouth than he saw the reflection of a wizened cowboy in the mirror behind him.

The man in the cowboy hat and boots stared at him with a measure of curiosity and compassion. Walker knew he looked like hell. Fearing the stranger would ask him what was wrong or worse, offer to help him—forcing Walker to tell him to mind his own business—he put the dime back in his pocket and left.

To his chagrin, the bartender nodded to him. Walker had no choice but to go over to the bar. He asked for a bottle of water. When the other man handed it to him, he put down a five-dollar bill. "Keep the change."

Outside the doors he rested against the wall and drank the contents before he went back to the motel. En route he stopped at the convenience store for a pack of gum. After the furnace he'd lived in for the past twenty months while deployed in Iraq, Markton's seventy-five-degree temperature felt cool to him.

The tail end of the dog walk was passing by farther down the street. Volunteers followed to do the cleanup. This was one event that must have been thought up while Walker had been in the military. After leaving his motel room earlier to get some fresh air, the kind you could only get at a 6,200 feet elevation, nothing could have surprised him more than walking into a dog parade.

Minus the six years he'd served in the Marines in various parts of the world, and the four years before that spent in Missoula, Montana, getting his college degree, he'd lived his whole life on the Cottonwood Ranch outside Markton. He knew the town as well as any other local, yet he'd never stayed at the old Rocking J Motel located around the corner before.

Built in the forties with few amenities, it would hardly be noticed, but it was exactly the kind of place Walker had wanted and needed on his return. For the moment all he required was a bed, a shower, an old TV that still worked to blot out the fragments of horror flying loose in his head, and *no family* except Jesse who'd always been his hero.

Thanks to the cooperation of his superiors, no one knew he'd been wounded, let alone that his service in the Marines had come to an end. That was the way he wanted it.

Once back in his room, he reached for the house phone. One of these days he'd be forced to get a cell phone, but not yet. He couldn't bear to be reached by anyone. Though he'd e-mailed the family to stay in touch, his older brother, Jesse, was the only one he'd talked to over the phone, the only one he'd felt like talking to.

Jesse was the ranch cattle manager and had their father's toughness, but he also possessed an innate kindness reminiscent of their mother. When the boys were growing up, Jesse was the one Walker looked up to and trusted. Over the years, that had never changed. Of course he loved his twin brothers and his sister, but they were younger. Right now he needed Jesse's wisdom and understanding if he was going to survive.

Answer it, Jesse. Please, God.

"Hello?"

His prayer granted, Walker sank down on the side of the bed in sheer relief. The familiar, forthright voice caused him to swallow hard. "Jesse? If you're not alone, don't give me away."

After a long, distinct pause, Jesse said, "I'm by myself in the truck on the way to the barn. Is it really you, Walker?" He heard joy in Jesse's words. It humbled him.

"Who else?" *What's left of me.*

"Where are you calling from?" Jesse asked.

The flashback had left his body trembling. "The Rocking J Motel." He couldn't believe there were still some old framed United Airlines Posters hanging on the maroon-and-yellow-flowered wallpaper.

More silence while his brother assimilated the news. "You've got to be kidding me! You're not really in Markton, are you?"

Walker eyed the motel key sitting on the bedside table. "Come to room fifteen and find out."

Jesse let out a low whistle. "You'll never know how much I've missed you." His voice shook. "I'll be right there!"

Walker closed his eyes tightly. Everything else in his world might be in chaos, but Jesse never changed, thank heaven.

After twenty minutes of pacing, he heard the sound of a truck pull up in the parking space outside the door. Walker moved a corner of the curtain aside in time to see his good-looking brother climb out of the cab wearing the white Stetson and checked shirt that were his signature. The thirty-year-old bull rider in the family didn't look any older than the twins!

His throat swelled with emotion as he stepped to the door and opened it. Their eyes met. Jesse's startling blue gaze examined him from head to toe, silently noting how the years had taken their toll on Walker.

"Go ahead and say it. It won't hurt my feelings. I look like somebody's idea of a nightmare."

Jesse's eyes glistened with tears he couldn't repress. "You came home. That's all that counts." He caught Walker in a fierce bear hug, causing his hat to fall off. "Are you back for good?" he asked in a thick-toned voice.

Walker's breath caught. "Maybe."

"What does that mean exactly?" Jesse demanded, relinquishing his hold.

He averted his eyes. "It means I'm out of the service. As for anything el—"

But Jesse didn't give him a chance to finish the sentence. He just hugged him again, harder. Though he was a couple of inches shorter than Walker, he could pack a wallop. Walker always thought his brother was bigger than life.

When they let go of each other, he noticed more lines of experience around Jesse's eyes and mouth, but thankfully everything else had stayed the same. With his short silvery-blond hair, another legacy from their mother, his older sibling always did stand out in a crowd. The ladies loved him, yet he'd managed to stay single. In that regard, he and Walker were a pair.

"I like the buzz."

"Ditto," Jesse answered with a smile, eyeing Walker's Marine cut before picking up his hat. He sat on one of the chairs set around the table and squinted at Walker while he twirled it in his fingers. "I take it no one knows you're home but me."

Walker snagged the other chair and flung a leg over to sit with his arms against the wooden back. "You've got that in one. I can't be around people yet."

"Understood. Hey, you know Grandfather Walker's cabin up on Carter Mountain is vacant. Is that far enough away for you?"

Jesse was reading his mind. Walker nodded. "But I won't step a foot in it if you don't agree to let me pay rent. I want that official and documented." He didn't need his father accusing him of not paying his own way.

"I'll leave a rental agreement on the table for you to sign."

"Thanks."

"What are you doing for transportation?"

"I'm taking care of it."

"Then you better pick up a couple of propane lanterns. The generator still works. I'll bring you the key later today along with anything else you might need."

He shook his head. "The key will be fine. I'll handle the rest."

His brother's expression sobered. "When did you plan to tell the folks?"

Walker made a noise in his throat. "I don't know." He looked away, then asked, "Are you competing somewhere tonight?"

"At the Stampede in Bakersfield. Dex and Dusty already drove the horses down. Dad and I are going to fly there late this afternoon and meet them. We'll fly home on Monday."

"In that case Dad won't appreciate a surprise from me right now." Live or die, the rodeo was the be-all and end-all of his father's existence. "I think it's best if I lie low until next week."

Jesse believed it, too. That's why he muttered in agreement. Walker loved him for that.

He cleared his throat. "How's everyone?"

"Good," Jesse said vaguely. "Walker—don't hate me, but you look ill," he blurted unexpectedly.

"Hey—I'm the walking wounded," he mocked. "You should see the ones who can't."

Jesse blinked back more tears. "Play the game with anyone but me. You used to weigh two hundred and twenty pounds. I can tell you're nursing your chest the way I did after Screwee Louee stomped on mine a few times. After that I started wearing a vest. Let me see what you've done to yourself."

"You wouldn't like the view. IEDs do a different kind of damage."

His brother's face lost color. "I *knew* it. Come on, little brother. It's time for show-and-tell."

Walker stood up and peeled off his white T-shirt. The cotton fabric was the least abrasive material against the skin grafts over his torso and left hip.

Another low whistle came out of Jesse. "How long were you in the hospital?"

"A couple of months. They've healed, but I keep thinking they haven't."

With a grimace, Jesse jumped to his feet. "What about the wounds on the inside? Who's seeing about those?"

Nothing escaped his brother. He put his shirt back on. "I'm scheduled to talk to a shrink at the VA clinic in Powell next week."

"Good." He chewed on his lip. Walker could tell he wanted to say he'd go with him, but thought better of it.

Time to change the subject. "How are you doing in the standings right now?"

"I had two pretty good nights last weekend at the Mesquite Championship."

"*How* pretty good?"

"An eighty-seven and an eighty-eight."

Walker slapped his brother on the back. "Not bad at all."

"We'll see what happens tonight."

"Who else is in contention that can measure up to you?"

"Robby Tedesco from Phoenix and Jake Seaton from Greeley, two younger dudes you don't know who are damn good. And then of course there's Mark."

Mark Hansen, a big, black-haired local from Markton who was part Lakota, had had an intense personal rivalry going with Jesse since their high school days. Some rivalries could be good-natured fun, but not theirs. "So he's still nipping at your heels after all this time?"

"Yup. He scored a ninety last week in Mesquite."

"I guess he's never been able to handle the fact you were world champion four years ago."

"He's figuring to beat me out before going all the way to the finals in Las Vegas come December."

Walker's brows lifted. "He can try, but it isn't going to happen."

Suddenly Jesse gave him another bear hug. "That's the kind of talk I've been needing to hear. Thank heaven you're back home." He finally released him. "I've got to go, but I'll be by later with the key."

"If I'm not here, just leave it with the office."

He saw more questions in Jesse's eyes, but he held back from asking them. "Got it."

"You're saving my life right now. You know that, don't you?"

Jesse nodded. "Look, Walker...I realize you don't want to see the family yet, but when I get back we're going to spend time together. I'm usually at the old arena before anyone else is up. I don't have to tell you what it would be like to practice with you again...."

"Maybe," he whispered. Walker hadn't been near an arena in over six years. The need to get away from his father had been all consuming. He'd decided to take his pain out of the country where he could try to blot it from his consciousness. The fact that several months before he'd gone overseas his best friend Troy, one of the top steer wrestlers in the state, had died in the box from a fatal concussion, had made it easier to leave.

"At least think about it. If nothing else I'd like you there giving me pointers only you can give. You'll be good luck against Mark." Jesse smiled when he said it, but Walker saw shadows in those blue eyes and was convinced Mark had burrowed deeper into his brother's psyche than anyone knew. The thought troubled him. "It'll be like old times."

No. Nothing could ever be like the old times. Guilt consumed him that he had to think way back to remember when he'd been truly happy. "I can't make any promises." *Not even for you, Jesse.*

So what kind of a monster did that make Walker?

"Right." He shoved his hat on his head in seeming resignation before heading out the door.

Once his brother had gone, Walker left for West Yellowstone, Montana, in his rental car. Instead of flying into Yellowstone Regional airport in Cody, he'd flown into the airport there three days ago. At the time he'd placed an order for a new black Ford Super Duty F-450 truck, which was now ready to pick up.

He didn't mind the two-hour drive from Markton to do business, not even with the steady stream of traffic. Until he talked to his parents, it was necessary to keep a low profile, and that meant staying away from the airport too close to home.

Once he'd taken possession of his truck, he bought all the items and groceries he'd need to move into the cabin. By midafternoon he was ready to head back to the ranch. On his way out of West Yellowstone, he stopped at a drive-through for a malted milk with a double cheeseburger and fries. The doctors had told him to force the calories in order to put on the twenty-five pounds he'd lost.

Though he couldn't finish all his lunch, he figured he was making progress. By the time he'd reached the ranch, taking the private road used by the Spurling Natural Gas Company to fill their trucks on land the Codys leased to them, he still hadn't thrown up. To his amazement he even tolerated a Snickers bar. The chocolate tasted good. It surprised him, considering how sick he'd been after his flashback.

His out-of-the-way approach to the cabin via the dirt road reminded him he'd returned to God's country. There were times in the past six years when he'd wondered if he would ever see this vista again. Its beauty robbed him of breath.

Twelve-thousand-foot Carter Mountain jutted in the air ahead of him. He'd climbed it countless times with his brothers as each raced to get to the top first. The boundary of the ranch ran all the way up into the Shoshone National Forest near the summit where the water drained into the south fork of the Shoshone River. Above the highest peak, the sky blazed as brilliant a blue as the moisture-filled gaze of the woman at the parade.

He'd recently left a land of people with dark eyes and hair. In the sun, her hair swirled ash-blond with a sheen like fine corn silk. The feathery cut brushed her neckline, a style he decided suited her curvy figure, even though he'd only glimpsed her for a moment.

She's a mother and someone else's wife or significant other, Cody. Forget what you saw.

Until he got a grip on his PTSD, he wasn't fit company

for himself, let alone a woman. No female would be thrilled to learn he'd been exposed to a chemical agent and might possibly be sterile.

Once Walker reached the cozy two-bedroom cabin nestled in the firs at nine-thousand feet, he jumped down from the cab, startling a white-tailed deer that pranced off into the pines.

His grandfather Walker, who'd died a year before Walker was born—and for whom he was named—had built this place in the '40s to enjoy nature with his family. It included a loft where the little kids could plop their sleeping bags and pretend they were camping out. He'd refused to put in electricity, clearly a man after Walker's heart.

He remembered his grandmother with affection. Joanne Cody had lived until he was eight years old. She was the one who'd helped him spot bobwhite quail and track the raccoons. When the antelope appeared, she'd round him and Jesse up so they could watch their movement through the binoculars. In the fall she'd point out elk and mule deer to their delight. The memories continued to bombard him. Ghosts from the past.

There was still an hour of daylight left. Before he got busy settling in, he took a long walk around the property to breathe in the remembered essence of his surroundings. The spruce trees in the front yard had grown taller and fatter. A family of jackrabbits heard him coming and leaped away, causing him to chuckle. He couldn't remember the last time he'd been even slightly amused.

From this altitude, which was more like being in a low-flying aircraft, he could see 2,500 head of Angus cattle grazing and take in part of the ranch's layout far below. The paved roads connecting the barns and arenas formed an interesting crisscross pattern he'd always found fascinating. With its dozens of outbuildings, including an airstrip bisecting the property, it resembled a small city. But dominating it all was the new fifteen-thousand-square-foot ranch house.

Like a pharaoh who'd ordered a pyramid constructed to his glory, his father had outdone himself. His mother had e-mailed him pictures, but seeing it in person for the first time left him at a loss for words.

The best he could come up with was that it reminded him of an immense, modern version of a baronial mountain lodge he'd once seen in Bavaria. Its common rooms rose in the center three stories beneath timbered beams. Most spectacular were the huge, diamond-shaped windows. They achieved a geometric amalgamation of dark honey-colored wood and glass.

With two floors of living quarters including eight bedrooms and an equal number of bathrooms, his father could assemble the entire family and entertain the world of rodeo aficionados in a style unequaled anywhere.

What truly impressed Walker were the grounds that had been left natural and provided the seamless blend between civilization and nature. If the landscaping had been pretentious, the whole picture would have been ruined.

Beyond his vision on the other side of the spread, fifty thousand acres were devoted to the natural-gas wells. It all looked perfect and beautiful, a testament to his father's incredible savvy as the ultimate rancher and businessman. No one could do it better. If the first Cody could see how Walker's father had taken care of his legacy, the tributes would be unending.

Walker chewed on a piece of sweet, wild grass as the sun slipped behind the mountain portending the advent of night, the time he dreaded most. Everything worked because his siblings revered their father and made it work. Every one of them worked hard and contributed to J.W.'s dream of being the greatest rodeo family of Wyoming.

Everyone except Walker…

Chapter Two

May 2

"Good morning, ma'am."

"Good morning." Paula smiled at the friendly, white-haired man who was probably the owner of Whittaker's Tackle and Gift Shop and had to be eighty at least.

"That's a mighty cute tyke you're holding."

"Thank you."

"Here's a little pinwheel on a stick for you, feller." He handed the toy to Clay who lost interest in the buttons on Paula's blouse and reached for it. "Now what can I do for you, young lady?"

She chuckled, not having been called that in a long time. "I'm looking for a gift that could be used as a paperweight, or maybe a good-luck charm of some kind. Possibly something in turquoise or another stone?"

Paula had been on her way to the Cottonwood Ranch when she'd seen the shop off the highway, patriotically bedecked with the Wyoming State flag and the U.S. flag in various sizes. On a whim, she'd pulled into the parking area.

"Is it for a man or a woman?"

"A man." An exceptional one in her opinion. That is if she could find him. She hoped she wasn't on a wild-goose chase.

"You might want something like this." He reached inside the counter and brought out a dark emerald-colored stone attached to a gold chain. It was shaped like a small leaf. "What you see here is genuine Wyoming jade made by a member of the Eastern Shoshone Tribe. You wear it around the neck for luck. Is this what you had in mind?"

It was the color of the stranger's eyes. She would never forget their unique hue. In fact she doubted she could reproduce it on canvas. The green would be like the color of the forest outside this man's store when the sun's rays no longer penetrated.

She noted the reasonable price on the little box before rubbing her thumb over the smooth surface. Clay tried to grab it with his other hand. "It's perfect." So perfect she couldn't believe it.

He beamed. "Shall I gift wrap it for you?"

"Please."

"Gold or silver paper?"

"Gold. Maybe some green ribbon?"

The man nodded. "How come you're clear out here?" He was a talker, but she didn't mind. He reminded her of her grandfather.

"I'm looking for a man who might live out this way."

"I know everybody in these parts and have outlasted most of them. What's his name?"

"I wish I knew, but I think he might be a Cody."

"Ah—you're talking one of J.W.'s sons. There've been Codys in Park County since 1904. They settled the choicest part of the South Fork Valley of the Shoshone. Cattle, coal mining—you name it, but between you and me they made their big fortune in natural gas. Nowadays they breed quarter horses."

Little did the old man know she was well acquainted with the mind-boggling Cody résumé, but she wouldn't have dreamed of interrupting him. He sounded like a publicist for the legendary Codys, whose ancestors had made their indelible mark here.

"Maybe you didn't know they're one of the first rodeo families west of the Continental Divide. John Walker was a champion until he got his leg stomped on. Now he has to use a cane. Tough as a buzzard. Keeps those boys of his in line. The daughter, too."

If Paula wasn't mistaken, one of his boys with short-cropped black hair and a lean, hard-muscled body had prevented a crisis yesterday, but *boy* was a misnomer. He'd met her criteria of a real man.

In case she'd been right and the stranger was a Cody, she hoped to meet him for a few minutes this morning so she'd have a chance to give him this small token in appreciation for what he'd done. But if she was wrong, she didn't want to bother J.W. or his wife, Anne, unnecessarily. She could find out the information she wanted by inquiring at the ranch office.

"Here you go." He put the package on the counter. She gave him her credit card. When the transaction had been made, he slipped the box in a sack and handed it to her. "Hope you find the Cody you're looking for."

"So do I. You've been very helpful."

"That's what I'm here for. Come back again."

"You can count on it."

In another ten minutes Paula turned into the entrance of the Cottonwood Ranch, passing beneath the giant arch of elk and deer horns. She hadn't been out here since late fall, but everything looked just as immaculate and prosperous as before. New buildings or old, she had to admit it took an iron hand to keep this ranching empire preserved in such A1 condition year after year. J.W. fit the role of the quintessential patriarch.

She drove to the parking area in front of the ranch office and turned off the motor. "Out you come again, Clay."

Leaving the pinwheel behind, Paula pulled her son from his car seat and looked around. There were half a dozen cars, trucks and rigs, some with horse trailers, parked on either side of the gravel drive.

She set Clay down with a kiss in his sweet-smelling blond curls and grasped his hand. Together they started walking toward the remodeled, log-cabin-style bunkhouse. After years of being exposed to the elements, the weathered gray wood formed a dramatic contrast to the backdrop of shiny, green-leafed cottonwood trees.

In the distance she could see the original homestead in the same log-cabin style up on a rise overlooking the river. More pockets of open-crowned cottonwoods maybe a hundred feet tall grew in clusters from thick gray trunks along the shore.

The first time Paula had noticed them, her thoughts had flown to the early pioneers who'd crossed the Great Plains needing the shelter and fuel these trees provided. She could only imagine their joy at discovering them. Surely the magnificent sight had inspired the first Cody drawn to this area.

If Paula had lived back then and had come upon this view, she would have said X marks the spot and immediately put down roots. In her contemplative mood, she hadn't realized Clay had stopped to pick up stones, making for slow progress. While she indulged him, it gave her a chance to concentrate on the rugged landscape rather than yesterday's close call that could have been an ugly, painful incident for her son.

Her gaze took in spectacular spires and pinnacles above sweeps of meadows as far as the eye could see. If she turned in the other direction she feasted on rolling foothills and forests of evergreens. Snowcapped peaks beyond the Shoshone River took her breath.

All of it belonged to one family....

A mix of cowboys was coming in and out the door. Two different men gave her an assessing glance and tipped their hats to her on the way to their vehicles. "Morning, ma'am."

She nodded before lifting Clay in her arms. "Let's get rid of these, shall we, little sweetheart?"

After removing the stones from his fists, she carried him up the steps and entered the reception area of the office with its rustic fireplace. Though she'd been in here before, she was struck once again by the showy, luxurious Western interior that demonstrated John Walker's power and wealth.

A collection of Western landscapes and rodeo paintings all in oils dominated two walls. Beneath them was a grouping of oxblood leather couches and a huge coffee table atop a massive buffalo rug.

While she waited to talk to the receptionist seated at the big desk on the other side of the room, she wandered toward one particular painting that had caught her eye before. The artist, whose name wasn't familiar to her, had captured the same view of the snowcapped peaks Paula had seen after getting out of the car. However, the painting's foreground showed a winter scene. There was no hint of the many summer greens hiding beneath the snow.

She shivered, glad it wasn't winter.

Her glance darted to the wall behind the receptionist, where she saw a large oil painting of two people. She hadn't paid that much attention before, but she did now. Her gaze narrowed on the plaque beneath it. Mark Cody 1870-1925 and Catherine Alder Cody 1880-1960.

Alder. Brent's folks in nearby Garland had neighbors who were Alders. Their ancestors had emigrated from Germany. This Alder woman in the painting, obviously the first matriarch of the Cody clan, had brownish-gray hair and looked liked many of the women of that early period who'd given everything to carve out a life here. Widowed, she'd lived thirty-five years longer than her husband.

Paula couldn't help but wonder if the same fate awaited her.

A full black beard and moustache camouflaged a portion of Mark Cody's strong-boned features. Probably from England or Wales—she didn't know for sure—he was a big hulk of a man who wore a fringed buckskin jacket, reminding her more of a mountain man than a settler.

She studied him for several minutes, intrigued by the spirit inside him. Few people had the vision to build a dynasty in this rugged country, an area once populated more by Plains Indians than the white men who began to intrude on their remarkable culture.

Clay started to squirm. "Okay, I'll let you get down." She lowered him to the floor and they moved closer to the desk.

"Good morning. Can I help you?"

"I hope so. I'm Paula Olsen and—"

"That name sounds familiar," she broke in, "but I don't recall meeting you before."

"No, we didn't meet. I was the landscape architect when the Codys built the new ranch house a few years ago."

"Of course. You did a wonderful job."

"Thank you. As a matter of fact I'll be doing a little more work for Mrs. Cody this month. She wants me to find her a place where she can plant a garden of bulbs."

"She *loves* flowers."

"Don't we all."

"That's a darling little boy you've got."

Paula smiled. "I'll keep him. In fact it's because of him I'm here." Without preamble she launched into her story of what had happened at the dog parade the day before. "I heard a man in the crowd say that it was John Walker's son who intervened. I tried to run after him and thank him, but he disappeared."

"No wonder you're eager to find him."

"The trouble is, I never met J.W.'s sons and don't know his name."

"Well, it had to be Jesse or one of the twins, Dex or Dusty. At the moment they're in Bakersfield at the rodeo stampede. What did he look like?"

"He was lean, maybe six foot three with the same black hair as his ancestor's in that painting behind you, but he wore it very short."

The woman looked puzzled. "That description would fit Walker, but it couldn't have been him because he's in the Marines fighting somewhere in Iraq at the moment. Was this person heartbreakingly handsome?"

All Paula saw in her mind was a dark, brooding image of a man with secrets. But she supposed that if he ever smiled, he could be described that way. "He was attractive," she murmured.

"Now you've got me intrigued. They say everyone has a double."

Paula closed her eyes for a second. Maybe the receptionist was right. "That must be the explanation," she said, yet she didn't quite believe it. Maybe Walker Cody was back on American soil and this woman didn't know about it yet. The man in yesterday's crowd had sounded certain the stranger was a Cody.

If he'd been in Iraq, then he'd seen and experienced unspeakable things. She'd gotten a tiny taste of it during her first phone call from Brent, but in subsequent calls and e-mails he'd refused to open up to her. It still hurt that he'd deliberately kept that hellish part of his life apart from her. She'd wanted to share it with him as they'd shared everything else, but it didn't happen.

"Sorry I couldn't have been of more help," said the receptionist, bringing Paula back to the present.

"But you were. Thank you for your time." Other people had entered the office and were waiting.

"Sure."

After coming all this distance with Clay, Paula was disappointed not to have caught up with the man, whoever he was, but there was nothing more to be accomplished here. Right now Clay was getting restless.

As soon as she got back to her apartment, it would be time for his lunch and afternoon nap. He would need a good one. After he woke up, she and Angie were taking the children to the park. Later on, Angie's younger sister, Katy, was going to tend them while Paula and Angie went to an early movie, their first in ages.

AS HE'D HOPED, WALKER only noticed a handful of people in the Markton cemetery at five in the afternoon. With his brothers and father in California, he didn't need to worry that someone would recognize him.

He'd been one of the pallbearers for his best friend's funeral six years ago and knew where to find his grave on the east end. Once he'd seen him buried, Walker had wanted to put the sorrow of loss behind him and hadn't revisited the cemetery. Later on he'd left for officers' candidate school, so he never saw the marker.

Coming closer to the area in question he spied a light granite stone with the outline of a rodeo rider on his horse. Troy Anderson Pearsoll, Beloved Son. Beneath Troy's name were the dates of his birth and death.

With tears in his eyes, Walker hunkered down and put the jar filled with baby blue eyes against the marker. A whole hillside of the wildflowers grew at the back of the cabin. They wouldn't last long, symbolic of his friend's life having been cut short the night of the Cody Roundup. But while he'd been alive, he'd brought color and excitement to Walker's life.

"What happened to you wasn't fair," he said, hoping Troy could hear him. He swallowed the sob in his throat. They'd been friends from elementary school on.

A myriad of memories flooded his mind. How many times had he and Troy practiced their steer wrestling before riding their horses up to the old cabin with a girlfriend hugging their waists?

They were crazy and cocky back then, and thought they were hot stuff. There were moments of pure joy, the kind you experienced in those teenage years when you believed you were immortal. That time would never come again. Thank heaven for those precious memories.

"I've missed you, buddy."

"I've missed *you*, Captain Cody," came a gentle voice behind him.

Startled, Walker looked over his shoulder to see Troy's mother holding a large pot of yellow mums. "Ruth!" He sprang to his feet.

The dark blonde woman studied him with moist, loving eyes. "I looked forward to every e-mail you sent, but seeing you here is the best thing that's happened to me in six years."

He took the flowers and placed them next to his before hugging her. She reciprocated with surprising strength. It was all he could do not to break down.

She wiped her eyes. "When did you leave the hospital?"

"Four days ago."

"So the Marines won't be seeing you anymore?"

"No."

"That's good. You're thinner and drawn, but somehow

you're even more handsome. Once you're bulldogging again you'll be better than ever."

If he thought it would help him get back to some kind of normal, he'd do it. Walker darted her a brief smile. "And you're prettier than ever. How's Leslie?"

"You know my husband. He's still at work and keeps busy." Troy's father owned the Markton Feed and Grain Store. "We both do now that Lynette's just had her third baby. A girl this time."

"That's exciting." If Walker could be thankful for one thing, Troy hadn't been an only child. His parents hadn't lost everything when they'd lost him.

"Your parents must be overjoyed you're back."

His body tautened. "They don't know yet. I'll call them tomorrow. Jesse's the only one I've told."

"You always were closest to your older brother." Her expression sobered. "Would you tell me something honestly?"

"Of course."

"Once a long time ago, Troy overheard his father say something to me that I've regretted and I'm afraid he told you."

He drew in a deep breath, knowing exactly what it was. "You mean the rumor he heard floating around the feed store about my dad having had an affair after he and Mom were married?"

Her face was a study in pain. "Then Troy *did* tell you. Oh, Walker, I'm so sorry about that. I've suffered over it for years, fearing it colored your thinking about your dad." She put her hands on his arms for a brief moment. "Neither Leslie or I would ever have said or done anything to hurt you. You always will be like another son to us."

"I know that, Ruth, and I'm honored by it, but I won't lie to you. It did affect me, but only because I've had issues with my father from the time I took my first steps and he insisted I could ride a horse. He had and still does have this dark side to him that doesn't allow for weakness in other people. Everything must be his way. He's a driven man where the rodeo is concerned. All or nothing.

"One night we had a rousing fight. I told him I didn't want to enter a certain bulldogging event because I had plans with Amy for the Riverside High School prom. He lit into me about letting girls get me off track.

"I was so angry, I took off riding with Troy. While I was spouting my venom for the hundredth time, poor Troy was trying to help me understand my dad's psyche. That's when he told me about what he'd heard. It shed a whole different light on the dynamics in my family."

Ruth looked stricken. "But it was only a rumor."

"Was it?" he fired at her.

"You mean you're still not sure one way or the other?"

He shook his head. "No. I've never discussed it with anyone, but I've had six years away to think about it. There's definitely something wrong between my parents. They're not like you and Leslie. Theirs isn't an easy relationship even though they appear devoted to each other. Dad's so rigid, I have to believe there's a hidden reason."

"I feel terrible about this."

Walker put an arm around her shoulder. "Please don't torture yourself about it anymore. I happen to know neither you or Leslie has a mean bone in your body. Troy wouldn't like it to see you this upset over something that wasn't anyone's fault. Life's too short."

She sniffed. "You're right. I'm so glad I saw you. What a coincidence! After spending the afternoon with my cousin out this way, I decided now would be a good time to visit."

He smiled. "It was meant to be."

"I think so. Thank you for being here to remember him. It means the world to me. When you find a minute, please drop by the house. Leslie will be thrilled to see you."

"I promise I'll come. You take care." He kissed her cheek before he left her to commune with Troy in private.

Walker strode toward his truck in a distinctly different frame of mind than when he'd driven down from the cabin. The thing about his father that had been festering deep in his soul for so many years had now erupted into an open wound. By no means could he ignore it.

Before he left for the cabin, he had one more errand to run in Cody. J. J. Callahan carried cowboy hats and boots. If he was going to start steer wrestling again, he needed both. In fact he'd better begin by breaking in a pair tonight.

"WHAT DID YOU THINK of the movie?" Angie asked as they filed out of the theater onto the street.

"A bit cheesy."

"What do you mean 'a bit'?"

They both chuckled. "I don't mind. It was nice to sit through something for two hours with no interruptions."

"Amen."

They had to walk down to the corner to reach Angie's car. Before long they'd passed several storefronts. In the distance Paula glimpsed a tall, lean cowboy in a black cowboy hat coming out of Callahan's. He was headed toward a black truck parked right outside and was obviously in a hurry. There was something about the way he moved...

Her heart beat faster. "Mr. Cody?" she called to him. He checked his stride to glance her way. So he *was* home from Iraq! "Just a minute. Please—"

She darted up to him, noting his dark blue button-down shirt and jeans. He was even taller in cowboy boots, powerful looking. His five o'clock shadow added a sensuality to the hard lines of his facial structure, yet he had a gaunt, almost forbidding appearance that intimidated her. Beneath the rim of his Stetson, his eyes looked black beneath black brows.

"Y-yesterday you didn't stay long enough for me to thank you the way I wanted to," she stammered like a fool. "If you hadn't grabbed Clay when you did, I don't even want to think about what would have happened."

"Neither do I," he muttered in a deep masculine voice that reverberated to her insides. "I'm glad any injury was averted. Now if you'll excuse me—"

Before she could take another breath, he'd climbed in the cab with unconscious male agility and started the powerful engine. In another few seconds he'd backed out and had taken off.

"Whoa."

She turned to Angie. "Whoa is right. I realize he was in a hurry, but I'm beginning to get a complex. That's twice now."

"It's not you. Trust me," her friend assured her, "and I meant 'whoa' as in, have you ever seen anyone as incredible? Drop-dead gorgeous doesn't even come close."

That's what the receptionist at the ranch office had said yesterday, but long, tall and deadly might be a better description. Unfortunately Paula was too upset by his swift dismissal to process everything. Maybe his behavior hadn't been of a personal nature, but she'd felt very much de trop just now.

They finished walking to Angie's Honda and got in. With people still returning to their cars after the film, she was glad they were leaving. Somehow she couldn't pass off the incident as nothing.

"Want to talk about it?"

She sucked in her breath. "There's nothing to say. I got his message. He's been thanked and from now on, no more thanks, thank you very much."

"What about the gift you bought him?"

"Absolutely not. The man made his feelings so clear I'm

still reeling. I'll put the jade away in a drawer as a gift for someone else one day."

"I understand." Paula appreciated Angie not arguing with her. "You worked with J. W. Cody a few years ago. Do the two of them seem alike?"

She stared blindly out the window. "No, but then his father was probably on his best behavior around me. I wouldn't know what he's really like except that he's myopic when it comes to the rodeo. If his son takes after him, then I guess there's a dark, primitive side to J.W. I'd just as soon not know about."

"Primitive? That's a pretty strong word."

"That's how he came across to me tonight." Yesterday he'd been a hero. Tonight he'd been…someone else, disturbing her on an elemental level that was unnerving. Was it something the war had done to him? Would Brent have come home affected in the same way? She shuddered, needing to put this whole incident out of her mind.

The fourplex where they lived was located on the east side of Cody. They'd left the west strip, but it was fairly slow going with all the traffic. Paula was anxious to get home to her son. Right now she needed his sweet, safe, unqualified love.

A sigh came out of Angie. "Don't dwell on what happened tonight."

"I won't. I've got to work up a design for the vice president of the Spurling Natural Gas Company. He wants the grounds around their headquarters relandscaped. After I put Clay to bed tonight, I'm planning to get busy on it. When I'm immersed, everything else goes out of my head."

"Lucky you."

Worried for her friend, Paula said, "Is your boss still giving you problems?"

"I'm afraid so."

"She's threatened by you."

"I know, but I need a job so I'm trying to keep a low profile. No matter what I do, it's wrong."

"Then you need to find another one, Angie."

"Actually I'm thinking about going back to college in Laramie to finish up my nursing degree."

"Good for you and horrible for me." They smiled at each other.

"If I can get a student loan, I might do it. As you know, my sister Marla lives there and would help me out with Danice. I'm going to have to make a decision quick if I hope to start summer semester."

"What about Ken?"

"I guess I didn't tell you he's got a new girlfriend."

He'd divorced Angie after getting involved with another woman. It was too pathetic. "I'm glad you're starting to think about your life and what's good for you. I'll help out any way I can."

"You already held me together through my divorce. What would I do without a friend like you?"

"I was just thinking the same thing about you." The thought of Angie moving made Paula's heart ache. Besides Paula's family, her friend had been there for her when Brent had left for Afghanistan. After the military had come to her door, Angie had seen her through her grief. They'd shared so much. Paula loved Danice.

"What about the Western Art Show in July? Have you started on something for it?"

"Not yet. No inspiration."

Angie turned to her. "That doesn't sound like you."

"I've been going through a dry spell. It's called artist's block," she joked.

"It's called you're depressed and don't have anything exciting going on in your life."

"I thought we did something pretty exciting tonight and look what happened."

They pulled up into Angie's parking stall. "You said you weren't going to think about the mysterious Cody son anymore."

"I'm not."

"Liar. Something tells me that man has broken a zillion hearts. Be careful he doesn't steal yours when you're not looking."

"Didn't you notice? He's not interested, and mine died."

Angie undid her seat belt. "One of the most amazing things I learned during my first year of nursing was the power of the body to regenerate after a loss. My husband left me, and yours got killed. Our hearts underwent a mighty wallop, but they're resilient, Paula. They're still beating, which makes them vulnerable again."

Paula got out of the car. "That's the last thing I want to be." The pain of losing Brent had been too devastating. "Spare me going through all that again. I couldn't do it."

"When I first found out Ken had been unfaithful, I felt like you. But not anymore. Life was meant to be lived. I intend to live it and not look back."

"I'm glad you feel that way, Angie. With your positive outlook, I know you'll meet someone wonderful."

She smiled at Paula. "I live in hope. Shall we find out if our little angels are sleeping?"

They went inside Angie's apartment. Within ten minutes Paula was back upstairs in hers. Clay had only wakened for a moment, but the second she put him in his crib he was out again. After kissing his cheek, she went into the kitchen for a soda.

Too strung up to go to bed yet, she checked her answering machine for messages. There was one from her mom, another from her brother, Kip, and one from her latest client.

"Hi, Paula. It's Matt Spurling. Not having to be in the office this morning has given me some free time at home. I thought over what you said about there being three votes before any work goes ahead on the landscaping, mainly yours, mine and a third party's. So I sat down with our vice president, Bob Javitz.

"Between the two of us we came up with that wish list you were talking about. You said to dream all we wanted and have fun making it. That's what we did."

Paula had already done the planning for the project with an engineer. But until she went over Matt's list, she couldn't draw up the design.

"I'm wondering what night you're free. I'd like to take you to dinner and discuss it with you. Maybe this Friday? Call me at your convenience. I'm looking forward to working with you. Talk to you later."

There were working dinner dates and then there were working dinner dates with more in mind than the business at hand. She was quite sure Matt's suggestion fell in the latter category. He was dark blond, good-looking, maybe mid-thirties and divorced. Nice. Tomorrow she would phone him to make arrangements, but it would be for business only.

Still unable to settle down, Paula almost wished Clay were awake. She longed to hold him and sing to him until his eyelids fluttered closed. She needed a reminder of Brent to blot out another image that seemed to have taken over. One that was so arresting, she found she could hardly catch her breath.

Chapter Three

May 4

Tuesday morning Walker rolled out of bed after another nightmarish night, realizing he couldn't put off the call to his mother any longer. It wasn't fair to Jesse, who was having to keep Walker's homecoming a secret from the family.

Before he did that, however, he needed to confirm his Wednesday appointment at 11:00 a.m. at the VA Clinic in Powell. It would only take a half hour to get to the college town northeast of Markton.

He made some instant coffee before straddling the bench of the pine picnic table on one side of the kitchen. While he looked out the picture window at the Indian paintbrush just coming into flower, he made his first call on the cell phone he'd purchased yesterday in Cody. Only the word *Unknown* would show up on the caller ID.

The receptionist told him he'd be seeing a Dr. Bader for a psychiatric workup per the arrangement with his physician at Bethesda. Just hearing that caused him to break out in another cold sweat.

I'm a nut job!

He slammed down the phone not realizing his strength. It cracked the display and made a little gouge in the varnished tabletop. When he tried to get a dial tone, nothing happened.

"Oh hell!"

He shot up from the bench and paced the red linoleum. His hand went to his face, reminding him it hadn't seen a razor in a week. He'd looked like the devil the night the blonde woman from Markton had singled him out in front of Callahan's. He looked even worse now. After making his purchases, he'd hurried back to his truck for fear someone would recognize him and tell the family.

It had shocked him to hear her call out his last name. Ever since that episode, he'd wondered how she knew. Once again he hadn't given her the time of day. Guilt gnawed at him that he'd been forced to be unconsciously rude to her, especially when he was more troubled than ever by the soulful look in those fabulous blue eyes.

In his gut he was positive they'd never met before or he would have remembered. You didn't forget a face and body like hers. He had no way of knowing if she was a local, or had come from somewhere else in Wyoming or out of state to vacation or visit relatives.

She wasn't wearing a ring. He hadn't noticed her with a man either time, but that didn't mean there wasn't a husband or a lover in the background. Her little boy was evidence of that. Walker didn't like the fact that he couldn't get her off his mind. The odds were against him ever seeing her again in passing, so to give her any more thought was absurd. He had something else pressing on his mind.

With his phone out of commission, he had no choice but to drive down to the ranch house and get this reunion over with in person. If his father was there, too, so be it.

He made a bologna-and-cheese sandwich with mayonnaise, consuming it on the way to the bathroom. A half hour later he emerged clean-shaven from the cabin in his new cowboy boots. He'd dressed in Wrangler jeans, two sizes smaller than he used to wear and a long-sleeved navy plaid shirt.

Another month of growing his hair out and he wouldn't look like the Marine's poster boy anymore. A cowboy hat had its uses. He'd always been partial to black. Jesse preferred white. Walker couldn't help but wonder if that's how their father saw his two oldest boys. No doubt when he discovered his number-two son had been back since last week without informing them, his estimation of Walker would degenerate to a new low.

Walker started up the truck and descended to the 7,500-foot level before the dirt road came out on pavement. He made a left turn and headed for his parents' ranch house magnificently situated on an undulating rise. Evergreens spotted the landscape. Closer now he saw ornamental trees and a profusion of flowers bordering the emerald grass outside the front entry. Once again he marveled at the perfection of the landscaping. It was as if the house had sprouted from the earth as naturally as the flora.

He pulled his truck into the parking area around the side next to a couple of cars and a new silver Chevy Avalanche. Something told him that was the truck his mother used to get around the ranch these days. Hopefully it meant she was inside.

His dad never drove anything but a Dodge Ram with the Cottonwood Ranch logo. He could be anywhere, but was probably at the office. If the family still operated the way they used to, the front door would be unlocked.

Sure enough it gave when he opened it. The first thing he saw was a larger-than-life-size bronze figure of a male rodeo rider on a horse. His father, an example of human hyperbole, had to have been the one who'd dreamed this up. Walker had already decided the landscaping was perfect, but the focal point of the massive, slate-tiled foyer was over-the-top.

He walked around it, then paused on the bottom step of the prominent staircase. It divided two-thirds of the way up to reach the east and west wings of the second floor. In a quandary, he realized that if he searched for his mother, it would startle her too much. Rather than ring the doorbell he called out, "Hello? Anyone home?"

Within seconds the sound of someone running broke the tomblike silence. In anticipation that it was his mother, his heart pounded harder. Soon the housekeeper who'd been with the family for years came hurrying out of a hallway behind the stairs. When she saw him, she came to a standstill. "Walker Cody—"

He smiled at the wiry, brown-haired woman who had a few more streaks of gray since he'd last seen her. Taking a step, he put an arm around her. "How are you doing, Barbara? You look well."

"I'm fine," she said, giving him a hug back, "but you're too thin. If your mother doesn't know you're home from the war, you'd better let me go upstairs to the bedroom and tell her so she won't have a heart attack."

"I'll follow you and wait outside the door." She nodded before starting up the stairs ahead of him. "You've stayed nice and trim, Barbara. Must be from having to keep this mammoth place in running order."

When they reached the east wing she smiled at him. "This house and three others."

"What do you mean?"

"Well, after your folks moved in here, three of the kids remained at the old homestead, and then there's Dusty's apartment over the barn and of course Tom's and my cabin beyond the old arena. These days I have a couple of maids to help."

There'd been changes....

She led him along the hallway to the first door that was slightly ajar and tapped on it.

"Come in, Barbara." The sound of his mother's voice took Walker back years. It had a soothing quality, easy on the ears.

"Are you prepared for company? There's someone here to see you."

"You mean someone's downstairs?"

"Not exactly."

Walker couldn't wait any longer before he entered the bedroom. His mother was bent over the side of the king-size bed where she'd laid out a paper quilt pattern to stencil onto fabric. She was famous for her homemade quilts. He'd watched her do this many times before.

Annie Cody, as everyone close to her called her, was a lovely woman, still trim in her jeans and Western shirt. Her hairdo was the same as before, a chin-length bob with heavy, forward-swept bangs from a deep side part. The only change he could see was that the color was more silvery-gray than blond now.

When she raised her head and their eyes met, she let out a heartfelt cry. Dropping her marking pen, she ran around the bed. He tossed his hat on the nearby table and met her halfway, picking her up to rock her in his arms.

"Mom..." he murmured, closing his eyes as he breathed in the familiar scent of the almond lotion she always wore. They hugged for a long time.

"Oh, Walker—" she broke down weeping "—I can't believe you're home at last." She clasped him harder. "It feels like you've been gone forever. Did you already stop at the office to see your father?"

"No."

"He's going to be overjoyed. Tell me this isn't just a visit. Tell me you're home for good."

"I am."

"Thank God!"

After he lowered her to the floor, she cupped his face in her hands. "Let me look at you." Her concerned blue eyes studied his features. "Even with the weight loss, you're still the most handsome thing alive. Thank heaven your life has been spared to come home to your family."

"As you know, a couple of my buddies didn't make it back."

"But *you* did!" She hugged him again. "Your room is ready for you down at the end of the hall. I tried to create your old—"

"Mom?" he interrupted her. "Before we do anything else, I'd like to talk to you for a minute. Please sit down."

"All right." She eased out of his arms. After wiping her eyes, she sat in one of the chairs near the huge diamond-shaped window. Their bedroom gave out on the same view he could see from the front of his grandfather's cabin. Only the elevation was different. Her hungry gaze examined him.

"Don't take this wrong, Mom, but I can't live here. You know that."

She clasped her hands together. "Because of your father."

"Because of him, because I'm twenty-eight years old and need a place of my own. Because I'm no good to anyone right now. For the time being I'm renting Grandpa Walker's cabin."

Surprise broke out on her features. Before she could ask how that had come about he said, "I called Jesse last week and he set things up for me."

Her eyes filled with tears. "Jesse knew all this time?"

"I'm sorry. I asked him not to tell anyone until I'd talked to you."

She sniffed. "I guess I'm not surprised you turned to him, but honey—the cabin's off the beaten path."

"You know I've always loved the cabin. I'd rather be there than anywhere. It's got propane and the big generator to keep everything running. That's all I need."

"But there's no one to take care of you. After returning from years of being in the military and all you've had to face, you shouldn't be alone. You need good food and someone to fix it for you. You need help to get back to your old life!"

"I'm aware of that, Mom." This was the hard part. "I just don't know about anything yet. I'll be getting therapy at the VA clinic in Powell on a regular basis. For the time being I can't tolerate being around other people. I was in a hospital for a couple of months before I flew home."

She blanched. "What happened to you?"

"I was injured in an explosion. Nothing serious or I wouldn't be here."

His mother looked horrified. "Why have you kept everything to yourself instead of letting us help you?"

"You couldn't have done anything. For what it's worth, the best way you can help me now is allow me to stay away until I've had time to adjust to being back. I get nightmares and other things."

"Don't try to spare me. You can say the words, Walker. You're suffering from PTSD and have flashbacks." The trained nurse in her was talking. "The worst thing you can do is isolate yourself."

He grimaced. "Give me time, Mom. Beyond my therapy, I'm doing a little fishing and hiking until I can figure out what I want to do with the rest of my life."

"Understood, but don't you forget the whole family wants to help you. They love you, Walker."

"I love them."

"You're going to need to talk about what happened to you."

"I know that, but for a while I have to be on my own."

"Will you at least let me give a party next week so we can welcome you home? How about Wednesday night? Just the family? They'll be here between rodeo events."

Walker knew it had to happen sometime. "Sure."

She took a deep breath. "When do you plan to tell your father?"

He shifted his weight. "I was hoping you'd do that for me."

His mother rose to her feet. "I'll do it, but I don't understand why you can't. If you only knew how he's been waiting for you to come home. He loves you and is so proud of you."

"Maybe that would be true if I were like the boys and Elly who have his same vision of things. But as you and I both know, I'm the proverbial black sheep in this family."

"That's not true! I don't ever want to hear you say that again."

"Spoken like a mother."

"Yes," she fired back. "One who loves you to pieces."

"I feel the same way about you, but we'll talk later." He made a move to leave.

"Wait," she cried as he reached for his hat.

"What is it?"

"I just remembered something. Doris told me Paula Olsen came by the ranch office on Sunday looking for you."

He frowned. "I don't know anyone by that name."

"Perhaps you don't remember my sending you an e-mail about the landscape architect from EarthDesigns in Cody. She worked with us and the architect while we were building the house. Doris didn't tell me until Monday. Paula wanted to thank you for saving her little boy from being bitten by a dog at the walkathon in Markton on Saturday. Is that true?"

Stunned by the news that his parents knew the mystery woman so well, he turned toward his mother. "It wasn't anything. I just happened to be walking on the sidewalk when I saw him tumble out of his wagon."

"Don't be modest, Walker. It wasn't a little thing."

"I wonder how she knew who I was?"

"I have no idea. Doris told her it couldn't have been you because you were in Iraq. She suggested Paula had seen your double and Paula left agreeing with her. Now it all makes sense. Of course she was grateful to you. After losing her husband, who died in Afghanistan, can you imagine her fright if her son had been bitten?"

She was a widow?

"I'm sure she'd appreciate a call from you, but of course that's up to you."

"Thanks for telling me, Mom."

He started to leave, but she grabbed on to him. "Walker… Before you walk out the door, won't you tell me what happened to make you push your father away so many years ago? I'd hoped that when you came home things would be different. There has to be an underlying reason for this breach. Can't you bring yourself to confide in me?"

His mother had finally given him the opening he needed. He looked down at her. "Let me ask you a question first." It was time to be up-front. Nothing else would do.

"Anything."

"Was Dad always faithful to you?"

Rather than a cry of righteous indignation in his father's defense, or even an instantaneous answer in the affirmative, the silence that followed Walker's question told him everything. Oddly enough, knowing the rumor had turned out to be true made little difference to him at this point. He'd lived with the possibility of it far too long.

It was no trick of light that her face suddenly paled and she averted her eyes. "Where did that come from?"

"If the answer is yes, it doesn't matter. If the answer is no, it still doesn't matter because the person who repeated the rumor to me is dead and buried."

To hurt the mother he loved without qualification was killing him, but she'd wanted the truth and so help him, he'd felt she deserved to hear it. Otherwise she'd always try to fix something that couldn't be fixed. With no more secrets, they could live and let live.

"I love you, Mom. Your loyalty to Dad is astounding. As far as I'm concerned you're a saint. Don't ever forget that. You know where to find me."

"Walker?"

"Yes?"

"Don't forget Wednesday."

He'd been positive she was going to say something else, then thought the better of it. At least his father's infidelity was no longer a matter of conjecture. That was something anyway.

"I won't." Giving her another hug, he left the house, his thoughts reeling with the knowledge that the person responsible for the landscaping was none other than the woman whose image hadn't left him alone.

Not wanting to run the risk of seeing his father, he took the road back to the cabin, but once he'd pulled up in front, he didn't feel like going inside. His mother's words still rang in his mind. Paula Olsen's husband had been killed in war.

Walker didn't want to think what her loss must be like. He'd seen Troy and two Marine buddies die and still felt the impact of those losses. But he hadn't lost a spouse. Her grief must be a constant well of pain.

After she'd gone to the trouble to try to thank him, the least he could do was seek her out and convey his sympathy. He had the strongest premonition that if he put it off, his psyche would find another reason to give him fits during the long hours of the night.

Without hesitation he started the engine and headed for Cody, taking the back way around the property to avoid people. Besides Jesse, Barbara had seen him and now his mother knew he was home. It wouldn't be long before the whole family buzzed with the news.

No doubt his mom was on the phone to his father, apprising him that Walker had returned. He had no idea if she would include the fact that their son had heard about the affair his father had covered up all these years. But if she stayed true to type, and he believed she would, she probably wouldn't say anything to him.

Though Walker had finally confronted her, he had no desire to discuss it with any of his siblings in the event they were clueless. In their case ignorance was bliss. Ruth Pearsoll wasn't the only one who wished Troy had never overheard the rumor and repeated it.

"PAULA? MR. CODY FROM the Cottonwood Ranch is here to see you. He doesn't have an appointment. What would you like me to tell him?"

Her heart did a swift kick. Did the receptionist mean J.W. or... Except that J.W. had never come to EarthDesigns. She'd always met him and his wife at the construction site of their new ranch house.

"Give me five minutes, Louise, then send him in."

If it was Walker Cody, she'd given up on ever seeing him again. Flustered, she reached for her purse and reapplied lipstick before giving her hair a quick brush. It was a coincidence that he'd found her in the office. She'd only come in long enough to meet with a new client and would be going back to the apartment in a few minutes.

With Angie home from work today, the two of them were trading off babysitting. When Paula got home, she would tend the children so her friend had some free time.

She'd barely put her purse back in the drawer when the attractive, disturbing man who'd filled too many of her thoughts walked in her office. Paula noticed he'd worn another shirt of mostly dark blue. Navy seemed to be his preference. No sign of a beard this morning.

As he removed his hat, she realized she'd been caught staring and got to her feet on unsteady legs. "Mr. Cody? This *is* a surprise. Won't you be seated, or are you in too much of a hurry?" The words had slipped out of their own volition, causing his facial muscles to tighten.

"I deserved that," he muttered in a grating voice without making a pretense of sitting down.

"It was rude of me to remind you," she apologized.

"*I* was rude," he came right back, "but it wasn't intentional."

"I—I'm sure it wasn't." Her voice faltered. "I take it the receptionist at the ranch office told you I'd come by to find out if you were the man at the dog parade."

He cocked his dark head. "Not directly. My mother was the one who conveyed the information. The e-mails I received from her while I was overseas contained nothing but praise for your work on the landscaping. Today I could see why. The monument my father erected would have failed if the setting hadn't been perfect. You have a gift, Mrs. Olsen."

The loaded statement told her so much she was aghast. One thing was perfectly clear. Walker Cody wasn't a man who would bother with a compliment unless he meant it.

"Thank you."

He studied her through enigmatic eyes. "Forgive me for

dropping in without an appointment and interrupting your work. I'd like a chance to talk to you, but not here." Since he wasn't a client, she didn't want it to be here, either. "If you'd give me your phone number, I'll call you."

Her pulse quickened. It appeared she was going to get the opportunity to thank him properly after all. She wrote her cell-phone number on the back of her business card and handed it to him. He took it without looking at it and slipped it in his shirt pocket.

"Until later," he murmured before striding out of her office on those long, powerful legs.

She sank back down in her chair, drained by a force she'd never come up against before. In her dazed condition, it shocked her when Louise's voice sounded through the speaker.

"Line two for you, Paula. It's Matt Spurling."

Who?

She shook her head to clear it. "Thanks, Louise." She pressed the button and picked up. "Hello, Matt."

"Good morning!" For this early in the day, he sounded too excited to talk to her. "I thought I'd better catch you to remind you about dinner Friday evening."

"I haven't forgotten." Angie's sister had agreed to babysit again. She was earning her money for her pep-club uniform in the fall. "I'll meet you at the Sunset House at six." It would probably be her luck that Walker Cody would choose that time to phone her. "If you have any more items for your wish list, bring them."

"I will. See you then. I'm looking forward to it," he added in a quieter voice.

"Designing the right landscape for a client is always exciting for me. See you then." She hung up after intentionally keeping the conversation professional.

It wasn't what he'd wanted to hear, but the truth was, she

still felt as if she was married and Brent was just away on a long trip. Paula's mother had told her she'd get over that feeling with time, but Paula couldn't imagine it, not after the kind of happy marriage she'd had with Brent.

As for Walker Cody, his appearance at her office had thrown her off balance because it was so unexpected. By noon she discovered she couldn't concentrate. Maybe she'd do better at home. Too full of adrenaline to sit there any longer, she grabbed her purse, turned off her computer and went out to the front desk. "Louise? I'm headed for home if Ralph is looking for me."

The older woman nodded. "I'll let the boss know. Was Mr. Cody here on business for his family?"

"Yes," Paula lied to avoid undue speculation.

"I didn't know a man that gorgeous was real."

Neither did Paula. The fact that she'd never heard Louise comment on any man before, despite the hundreds who'd come through these doors while Paula had worked here, didn't help her chaotic emotions. "His parents are attractive people. I would imagine it runs in their family. See you later."

Paula hurried out to her Toyota, not wanting to get into a further discussion of Walker Cody's looks. Louise had shown a lot of compassion after Brent died, but she had a tendency to gossip. Around the office, Paula preferred to keep her private life to herself and intended it to stay that way.

En route to the apartment her cell phone rang. She clicked it on without checking the caller ID and said hello. Though she doubted it would be Walker this soon after his visit, her heart rate sped up only to subside when she heard her mother-in-law on the other end. Alice wanted her and Clay to drive to Garland on Saturday and spend the day with the family.

Normally Paula would have said yes, but because she didn't know when Walker would phone and want to meet, she asked if she could get back to her. After they chatted for a few more minutes and said goodbye, Paula realized that in putting Alice off she was behaving exactly like a teenager hung up on a guy.

In those brief seconds when Walker Cody had acted at the dog parade, Paula had to admit something out of the ordinary had happened to her. With hindsight she recognized it for what it was. *Widow's hormones.* She'd heard about them—the insidious phenomenon that made fools of women whose baser instincts came out of hiding during their grief.

Strong physical attraction had a lot to answer for.

It couldn't be anything else. They'd barely met! Even so, it seemed an unconscionable betrayal of Brent's memory. Filled with guilt, she drove faster, anxious to get home to Clay.

AT THE END OF THE TWO-HOUR appointment on Wednesday, Dr. Bader wrote out a prescription and handed it to Walker. The mild-mannered psychiatrist, probably in his fifties, with thinning dark blond hair, had come as a pleasant surprise to him, probably because he didn't look like Walker's idea of the stereotype. "These are what we call a beta-blocker to cut down on the adrenaline when you sleep. They should help you get the nine or ten hours you need."

Walker couldn't imagine sleeping that long, but at this point he was ready to try anything.

"I'm here to help you and be your support, but I need to warn you about something. You may suffer from PTSD for the rest of your life, not to the degree or intensity you're experiencing now, but certain memories will stay with you for the rest of your life.

"The strategies I've suggested in this session will eventually help with the number and severity of your episodes. No smoking, no drinking, no tea, no coffee, no recreational drugs. Your nervous system and bloodstream need to be a hundred percent free of chemical agents that automatically set you off."

Walker nodded. He despised any kind of tea. Drugs and smoking had never been a problem. Denying himself a beer would be a form of deprivation, but he'd go along with the doctor for a while. Coffee was another matter. There was no substitute for it.

"The hiking you're doing is excellent. Keep it up. You've indicated your plan to get back to the rodeo. That will facilitate your recovery in a big way. The important thing is consistent exercise that gets your body moving. Don't forget five healthy meals a day in portions you can tolerate until you've put on the weight you lost. You ought to explore yoga and meditation. There are several places in Cody where you can sign up for classes."

"I don't know about that."

"Take a chance and try it. You might like it and find it relaxes you. Besides our weekly sessions on Wednesdays, I'd like you to attend our support group for vets. We meet on Tuesday and Friday nights. Since you're living alone, it's important you meet often with others going through the same thing so you don't think you're the only freak on the planet."

Bingo.

"Walker, you mentioned you're close to your older brother. Stay in touch with him every day. You need that bond with a loved one, even if you're not ready to open up. Keep in mind that through him the rest of the family will be helped. By doing this, you'll be relieved of a lot of guilt."

Guilt's my middle name.

"I'm giving you two drawing tablets and a couple of packs of pastels to get started on your art therapy. You'll eventually know if you'd rather draw with something else like pen or paint, even crayons.

"The point is, always keep one tablet for the cabin and one for your truck because there'll be times when you'll be driving and something will trigger a flashback. It might be a smell, a noise, an accident of some kind. At that moment you'll need to pull off the road to get control of yourself. One of the best ways to do this is to express what you're feeling on paper."

"I'm no good at art."

"You don't have to be. No one's going to judge anything. It's a form of expression to release the emotions inside you that you can't explain or put into words yet.

"When you're at the cabin and restless, start drawing what you see when you think of Iraq. Maybe it's a camel, or a desert, or a house or a native. Then color inside the outlines to get out your fear, your rage, your helplessness over the women and children you couldn't help."

He felt all those emotions and more.

"Every Wednesday when you come to your appointment I want you to bring these tablets and we'll examine what you've done. Don't throw anything away. We'll walk through the pictures so your right and left brain can start talking to each other."

Walker shook his head. "I can't see doing it."

"That's what everyone says until they go through the motions and it begins to take hold. We'll work on getting you reintegrated so you retain your skills. You need to become a whole person again and look at every aspect of your personality with appreciation and respect."

That would be the day.

Dr. Bader stood up. "We've accomplished a lot today. Let me know if you can make Friday's session. We start at 7:00 p.m. and quit at nine. Your family, your brother, or anyone else close to you—a friend or girlfriend—all will be welcome to join us. It'll be well worth your time.

"Keep one more thing in mind. Until you've decided on a career, the best way to make use of your time is to give service to any number of organizations or to one person who could use your individual help."

"I'll think about it." Walker rose to his feet and shook the other man's hand. "Thank you for your help, but I'm afraid you're working with a lost cause."

The older doctor eyed him compassionately. "That's what most returning vets say on their first visit with me. One of my patients came home from Iraq after surviving an ambush that took out eight of his buddies. In a word, he's an exploding ball of hate. But with therapy, he'll do much better."

With that sobering revelation, Walker left the clinic needing relief after the heavy session he'd had with the doctor. Paula Olsen's image always hovered in the background of his mind. His first act of service would be to offer his condolences to the widow whose husband didn't make it home.

Pulling out the new cell phone he'd been forced to buy, he reached for his wallet where he'd put her business card. With an urgency that surprised even him, he found himself calling her.

Chapter Four

May 5

Paula had just put Clay down for his afternoon nap on Wednesday when she heard her cell phone ring. Every time the music played she wondered, even though she'd ordered herself not to think.

Tiptoeing out of his room, she hurried to the dining room where she'd left her phone next to her computer. The caller ID said *Unknown,* which meant anyone could be on the other end.

"Hello?"

"Mrs. Olsen? Walker Cody here." His deep male voice penetrated to her insides.

Her pulse raced. "How are you, Mr. Cody?"

"I'll be better if you call me Walker. After learning you're on a first-name basis with my parents, it shouldn't be that difficult. Mind if I call you Paula?"

She clutched the phone tighter. "No. Of course not."

"Good. I've been in Powell and will be driving into Cody in about ten minutes. If I came by your office, would you be able to get away for a quick lunch so we could talk?"

So far she'd discovered him to be a spur-of-the-moment man. Now you see him, now you don't. If she wanted to spend even five minutes with him to give him the gift she'd bought, she needed to act immediately or live to regret her hesitation.

"I didn't go into the office today. Fortunately for me I do eighty percent of my work at home so I can be with Clay. Since he's just gone down for his nap, would you like to come by my apartment? I was just about to make myself a tuna-fish sandwich. How does that sound?"

It felt like a lifetime before he said, "I haven't had one of those in years."

"I take it that's a yes. I live in a fourplex on East Oak, number 368, south side of the street. My apartment is upstairs on the right."

"I'll be there shortly." He clicked off.

Galvanized into action, Paula hurried into the bedroom to change into a fresh cotton top in a pale pink color with short sleeves. She'd leave on her jeans. Luckily she'd showered and washed her hair that morning while Clay was still playing in his crib.

After applying a frosted pink lipstick and running the brush through her hair, she hurried over to the dresser where the little gift sat in the drawer. She took it to the kitchen and started fixing lunch. When everything was ready, she set the drop-leaf table with two place mats and put his gift next to his glass.

Paula heard his knock and appreciated the fact that he didn't ring the bell and wake up Clay. She knew she was flushed as she walked to the front door and opened it.

No cowboy hat shielded his cloudy green eyes today. He'd dressed in a gray T-shirt, jeans and cowboy boots. Paula decided that whatever he wore didn't matter. It was the man who captured her attention. *Every time.*

But no matter how attractive she found him, he wasn't Brent.

"Come in, Walker."

"Thank you." He moved past her, causing their arms to brush. She felt the contact as if she'd come up against a live wire. Shutting the door, she watched his tall, lean body move around the living room as he examined the landscapes done in watercolor covering the walls. They represented years of working at her hobby. None were framed yet.

She'd signed all of them so there could be no doubt who'd painted them. Brent had urged her to display them in a gallery, but when she realized he was never coming home, she lost interest in her artwork and concentrated on her career.

Walker finally turned to her, studying her even more intently than before. "With talent like yours, you could pretty much do anything. For the sake of my father's geometric monolith, I'm glad you went for a degree in landscape architecture."

A chuckle escaped. "So am I. Designing something for your parents was an exciting challenge."

In a deft move he reached for the framed, eight-by-ten photograph of Brent propped on one of the end tables. She'd taken it while he'd been dressed in his army fatigues before being deployed. His gentle smile and dancing blue eyes followed her wherever she walked.

"America's finest," Walker muttered before putting it back on the table. He turned to her with a haunted look marring his striking features. "Mother told me he was killed in Afghanistan."

She nodded, dry-eyed. "Time has helped me get over the worst of it."

"The hell it has," he challenged, rubbing his chest absently as if he needed to do something with his hands. His eyes looked savage. "The spouse of a fallen soldier suffers trauma no one who hasn't been there can begin to understand."

He'd bludgeoned through to the truth so fast, she gasped and turned away from him.

"I've said too much." His voice grated in self-abnegation.

The next thing she knew he'd bolted for the entry. She couldn't let him go. Acting on pure instinct, she placed herself between him and the door. "You didn't offend me, soldier," she said in a stern voice. His tormented face was only inches from hers. "In fact you're the only person I've met with the guts to call it the way it is. Don't leave…"

They stood there like two out-of-control combatants trying to catch their breath while they regrouped. He backed away from her as though he'd been stung.

"I'm not safe to be around," he whispered in a deadly tone.

"Why? Because you're honest?"

His jaw hardened like a piece of granite.

Paula had to think fast before he disappeared and never came back. "Clay's all I have left of Brent. I'm grateful the warrior in you came out on Saturday. Before I could grab for him, you snatched him away from danger." She smiled. "You were awesome."

Maybe she was getting through to him because the wild look slowly left his eyes. "On the phone you said you wanted to talk to me."

He shifted his weight. "Actually, I thought you might want to talk to me. When my mother told me you'd lost your husband in Afghanistan, I was reminded of the wives of two buddies in my unit who were killed in Iraq. They needed to talk to someone who'd been there.

"I may not have known your husband, but we all faced a common enemy under similar circumstances. If you're like their wives, then you need someone to scream at, or to cry to. I wanted you to know I'm available."

"Thank you. That means more to me than you could know. Eighteen months ago I would have taken you up on your offer. My initial rage has passed, but just knowing you've been to war like Brent makes it easier for me to be myself around you." And more wary of your incredible appeal. "I don't know about you, but I need to eat."

Paula started walking toward the dining room that led to the kitchen. It reminded her of the time when she was ten years old and her father had given her a new pony. She'd used every trick to get it to follow her. In the end she just walked away, and then the miracle happened.

The next time she looked, he was standing next to the high chair and taking up most of the space in her tiny kitchen. Relieved he'd made it this far, she filled their plates with sandwiches and potato chips and put them on the table. "Please sit down."

She waited until he did her bidding. "What's your preference? Tea? Coffee? Water? Juice? Milk? Chocolate milk?"

His black brows lifted in surprise. "You actually have chocolate milk?"

Aha. "Clay likes it. Of course I only give it to him once in a while. Today's your lucky day, Walker Cody." She pulled the carton from the fridge and poured them both a glass before sitting down.

On a whim she lifted hers in his direction. "To a brighter future." As she took a sip, he flashed her an inscrutable glance before he drank the entire contents of the glass in one go.

He proved far too fascinating for her peace of mind. She took a bite of her sandwich while he devoured his. It amazed her they'd made it this far and he was still here in her apartment. "Maybe my toast was premature and you're only home on leave."

After a moment he said, "I resigned my commission. Right now I'm living in my grandfather's cabin on the ranch."

So he wouldn't be going back…. The news shouldn't have mattered to her, but it did. She wondered why he'd gotten out of the service, but she'd never know unless he volunteered that information.

She watched his gaze drop to the package. "I'll always be grateful for what you did for Clay. There's no way to repay you, but I bought you a little gift anyway. Please…open it."

Wordlessly, Walker reached for the box and undid the wrapping. After removing the lid, he drew out the stone.

"It's a good-luck charm of Wyoming jade made by the Eastern Shoshone tribe. Your presence brought Clay luck. I'm hoping the charm will do the same for you."

When he lifted black-lashed eyes to her, they reflected the deep green hue of her present. "I've never worn jewelry. This will be a first. Will you put it on me?"

Her lungs constricted. When she'd bought it, she'd hoped he might wear it sometimes, but she never imagined doing the honors. Getting up from the table, she walked around and took it from his hand. There was an intimacy in the process of fastening the chain around his neck.

As she struggled with the catch, her fingers brushed his skin. He was such a beautiful man, her awareness of him was almost overpowering. "There."

Paula quickly moved to the counter and put some cookies on a plate, which she brought to the table. She didn't dare look at him for fear he would be able to tell how affected she was by what had just happened.

How could she be this strongly attracted to him when Brent had been her whole world? She despised this unexpected weakness in herself. "If I'd had enough time, I would have made a pie or something," she added lamely.

He bit into a cookie, then ate half a dozen. "I haven't had an Oreo in at least six years. Between these and the delicious lunch, you've put me in touch with some happy memories. When I left the VA clinic earlier today, I didn't know that was possible."

That's why he'd been in Powell. She was glad to hear he was getting help. If Brent had made it home, that's probably where he would be getting therapy, too.

"Watching you drink your chocolate milk will be a happy memory for me," she confessed. For the first time since she'd known him, he smiled.

Was this person heartbreakingly handsome? the receptionist at the ranch office had asked.

Right now Paula couldn't find the words.

Too soon the moment was gone. "I think I can hear your little boy." He got to his feet, signaling he was about to leave. She realized she didn't want him to go, but what he chose to do or not to do was out of her hands. The war had taught him how to survive. Now he was a man in flight from himself.

After clearing the table, he paused in the doorway. "Thank you for the gift and for putting up with me." He darted her an oblique glance. Then like a gust of wind that had blown itself out, he disappeared.

BEFORE WALKER LEFT CODY, he stopped at a local supermarket and picked up a couple of half gallons of chocolate milk. It could never replace coffee, but nothing had tasted so good to him in ages.

On the way back to the ranch Walker found himself feeling the smoothness of the jade piece several times where it rested against his chest. He didn't need the dime anymore. The talisman Paula had given him would serve much better. When she'd hung the chain around his neck, he'd felt the warmth from her body seep into him, bringing his senses to life.

In that moment while her fingers brushed against his skin as she fastened the clasp, he forgot she was still in mourning for her dead husband. All he knew was an overwhelming awareness of her femininity and his susceptibility to her touch. If he hadn't picked up the sound of her boy making noises, he might have grasped her hands and pulled her arms around his neck in order to feel more of her. How terrifying would that have been for her?

Throughout his military career Walker had enjoyed relationships with his share of available women, most recently a nurse at the hospital. But knowing they could never mean anything more to him when his roots were in Wyoming, he'd only seen them as distractions.

Paula Olsen came from another category altogether. She was a widow who was emotionally unavailable since burying her soldier husband. He'd seen the signs in his buddies' wives. This former wife had a son to raise. Her husband's son.

Any man wanting to get involved with her would have to deal with the ghost between them. Walker wasn't that man, particularly not when he was damaged goods.

Yet this out-of-control stranger had wanted to turn around and go back to her apartment because there'd been moments with her when he'd escaped from himself.

Ironic that for a precious few seconds she'd made him feel safe when no place was safe. Explain *that* if you can, Dr. Bader.

His shrink had told him to stay in touch with Jesse every day. It put a lot of responsibility on his brother. Too much. He'd set up Jesse to be the go-to person in the family for information. How fair was that?

Rather than engage him in conversation, Walker would go back to the cabin and e-mail him, letting him know he'd gone to Powell for his appointment. That would appease Jesse's fears.

As long as Walker was at it, he'd e-mail Dr. Bader and tell him he'd decided to be at the support group Friday night. If he were honest with himself, it wasn't a meeting he was looking forward to, but he knew he had to try and cope now that he was home.

ON FRIDAY EVENING PAULA let herself in the apartment and made a beeline for Clay, who was moving around on his sturdy legs from the chair to the couch. She plucked him from the floor and kissed him.

Katy got up from the couch. "He's so cute. I just love him."

"So do I. Thanks so much for sitting."

"I'm glad to do it."

Paula reached in her purse to pay her. "How did things go?"

"Just fine. He ate part of a banana and some Cheerios."

"You're such a big boy." She kissed her son again while she walked Katy to the door.

"Oh—I forgot. Soon after you left, someone rang your doorbell, but I didn't answer it."

"Smart girl."

"When I looked out the window, I saw this really hot guy get in a black truck and drive away."

Walker.

To her chagrin, her heart pounded off the charts. "It sounds like it was Mr. Cody from the Cottonwood Ranch where I'm still doing some landscaping," she said, attempting to sound businesslike. "He knows my number and can call me."

The rational part of her decided it was better that he'd come while she'd been at dinner with Matt Spurling. It was better for her peace of mind that the man who'd dominated her thoughts had come by the apartment while she was gone.

Her client had asked her out for next Friday night, but she'd told him she would be in Garland with her in-laws. On the drive home from the restaurant, he'd warned her he wasn't giving up.

"Well, I guess I'll head out," Katy commented, bringing Paula back to the present. "See ya."

"Be careful driving home."

"Don't worry."

After she left, Paula gave Clay his bath and put him to bed with a bottle. She was glad Matt had given her his wish list. It provided her with plenty to do to keep her mind occupied, but by ten after nine she gave up trying to concentrate and decided to go to bed with a good book.

When Walker had left her apartment the other day, she'd wondered if she would ever see him again. Though part of her thrilled to hear that he'd come by this evening, another part of her knew it was better to stay away from him.

Paula had been married to the love of her life and had lost him. She had no interest in getting involved with someone else and going through that again. And she had Clay to think about. Whatever reason had brought Walker to her door this evening, she told herself she was glad she hadn't been here.

No sooner had she turned down the covers than her cell phone rang. In case it was Walker, she waited until the third ring in order to sound composed.

"Hello?"

"Paula? It's Walker." Her breath caught without her volition. "I know it's late, but since you weren't home earlier, I thought I'd take a chance you were still up."

"I just got back from dinner." He didn't need to know it was for business with a client. It would be better if she didn't explain anything.

"Then you've had a long day. Under the circumstances I won't keep you. I came by earlier on my way to Powell for a group-therapy session with my psychiatrist. On Wednesday he gave me an assignment, but I didn't know where to start. Do you know anything about art therapy?"

Actually she did.

But she'd already had the talk with herself about the dangers of widowhood and her powerful physical attraction to Walker. Despite the fact that she'd been the one to start all this in order to thank him, she couldn't allow anything else to go on or she might start to care about him. He had baggage. So did she. She didn't want to deal with it or him, not when she would always love Brent. Already her guilt for fantasizing about Walker was eating at her.

Clearing her throat she said, "No one needs pointers for that as I'm sure you found out tonight. I hope the session went well for you, Walker."

A caustic laugh came through the phone. "Forgive me for disturbing you. Good night."

Her eyes closed tightly. Wrong thing to say to him. He'd just come from therapy. If Walker had needed to share some of his war experiences and had decided to seek her out, then she'd just shut him down.

As the line went dead, Paula clapped a hand over her mouth. What had she done?

FEELING AS THOUGH SOMEONE had thrown a double punch to his gut, Walker turned on his laptop and saw that Jesse had e-mailed him back. He leaned over the kitchen table to read it.

Hey, bro. I'm glad you've got a place to go in Powell where you can be with guys who understand you. I probably know you better than anyone, but I realize none of us at home can know the kind of hell you've lived through.

Everyone's dying to see you. I've told them you need your space, but I won't lie to you. Dad's having a hard time waiting for you to come to him. I realize that couldn't be news to you. I'm just preparing you for next Wednesday night's dinner.

I've caught Mom crying twice when she didn't know I was watching her. When they decorated the new house, she took special pains to make sure your room was exactly the way you'd want it. I could have told her she was wasting her time, but I didn't have the heart.

I'm not trying to lay a guilt trip on you. One thing I do know about a returning vet, only straight talk counts for anything, so that's what you'll always get from me. Love ya, bud.

Walker groaned before sending him a reply.

Love you, too, Jesse. You're the best.

He moved over to the sink and took his pill with the last of his chocolate milk. Stan, one of the vets from nearby Ralston who'd also had an appointment with Dr. Bader, suggested he try hot, sugar-free Tang as a replacement for coffee. He'd been home six months and it worked for him. Tonight when the session was over, Walker had picked some up at the store and would try it in the morning.

After brushing his teeth, he got ready for bed and turned off the lantern. It was a beautiful night. The stars would be out soon. He settled back against the pillow with one arm behind his head. His other hand went to the jade piece at his throat. He fingered it for a long time, willing it to bring him a modicum of peace, but not believing it.

You're not in Iraq, Cody. You're back on the mountain among all that's familiar, so why in the hell do you feel like a child whose nose is pressed against the glass, looking inside at a world you don't feel a part of? How could that be when this was the only world he wanted?

His turmoil grew more acute because he knew if he didn't integrate here, then he belonged nowhere. The cold sweat he dreaded broke out on his body. He threw off the covers, allowing his skin to breathe until he knew nothing more.

Saturday came. He hiked until he was ready to drop in the hope he'd pass out when he went to bed. It might have worked, but a rainstorm came up during the night. Around four in the morning a series of thunderclaps brought on a flashback. He flew into the living room breathing like a crazed animal before he realized he was in the cabin, alone and safe.

This latest flashback pretty well shattered any fantasy he might have had about bringing Paula Olsen up here. All she had to do was witness one and it would shock the hell out of her. After last night's fiasco of a phone conversation, the best thing to do where she was concerned was go cold turkey and never see her again.

While he was at war with his emotions, he heard a noise. One of the shutters on the other bedroom window was banging. The wind must have pried it loose. He got dressed and lit a lantern while he hunted for some tools. Then he went outside to take a look at the damage.

The storm had baptized the earth. Right after it rained, the smell of lupines and baby blue eyes was particularly strong. As he breathed in the fragrance, family memories assailed him from the most heartwarming to the most bittersweet, bringing his thoughts full circle to that black moment when the legs had been cut out from under him.

Just the possibility that Walker's father had been unfaithful to his mother had been so incomprehensible to him, so shattering, he'd been driven to leave the ranch. The instinctive need to lose himself had prompted him to join the military.

Jesse had begged him not to go, but he didn't understand the agony Walker had been in, and Walker couldn't tell him. He couldn't tell anybody. Jesse had assumed Troy's death had been at the root of his unrest, and Walker had let him think it.

The disappointment in his father *if* the rumor were true had created a demon that had gotten a stranglehold on him. It was the same demon that had worked on him during the war. Hearing the truth from his mother had torn him up all over again.

Using more force than necessary to make certain the hinge on the shutter was secure, he drilled some holes and drove in new screws, then he went back in the cabin for a shower and shave. After Walker got dressed in clean jeans and a T-shirt, he made himself some Tang. It was tolerable. He couldn't see it becoming a habit, but for now it would do.

Dr. Bader had spoken the truth. If you went home and dwelled on the things you couldn't change, you could plan to die emotionally. It was your choice if you wanted to live in the here and now.

For Walker to do that, he had to figure out where to start. Getting back to the rodeo was something familiar. It would feel good to get on a horse and see if he still had what it took to throw a steer, but that couldn't be the whole of it.

Remembering an idea he'd had in college that had caused him to switch from mining to natural-gas engineering, he got in his truck at sunup and took a drive to the other side of the ranch. When he reached the gas wells, he parked off road and got out to walk around.

The Cody family depended to a great extent on the revenue from these wells. They'd been doing their efficient job for a long time, but he'd done measurements with an expert as part of his senior-year project and learned that one day soon, the supply of natural gas in this field would be exhausted.

When that time came, their family needed to have plan B already in the works if they hoped to continue the lifestyle to which they'd become accustomed.

His brain teeming with ideas his father wouldn't find of value, Walker eventually got back in the truck and drove the length of the field to the untouched rangeland beyond. He sat there for a long time gazing out at the landscape, wondering what lay beneath it. Eventually hunger broke his concentration, forcing him to drive back to the cabin.

One good thing: his appetite had returned. Dr. Bader's list of dos and don'ts was working. The only thing it didn't have on the don't side Walker had already figured out for himself.

Don't let Paula Olsen into your life.

"LOOK AT ME, CLAY," the photographer called out, dangling a cute little duck in his hand. "Give me a smile."

Clay wouldn't look up even when the man made it quack. Paula groaned. When she and Angie had decided to meet at Wal-Mart after work to get pictures taken of the kids, she'd thought it was a good idea, but the place was crowded and Clay refused to cooperate. It was a shame because he looked so adorable in his new turquoise-and-white shirt and shorts with the fish on them.

She shot Angie a vexed glance. "How come Danice was an absolute angel through the whole shoot?" Other mothers were standing in line with their toddlers, anxious to get their pictures taken.

Her friend laughed. "They sure pick their days."

"Well this one has already done me in." She kissed Clay. "Come on, sweetheart. Just a little smile for me?"

"I have an idea," the photographer said. "Hold him while I get something out of the back room. This usually does the trick when all else fails."

She and Angie exchanged amused glances while Clay kept pressing kisses to her face. Within seconds the man returned with a black bear bigger than her son, the kind sold in every tourist trap throughout the state.

"Here we go! With Mommy's help you can ride him."

Clay took one look at it and let out a terrified shriek. Suddenly he was hysterical and tried to bury his face in her neck. His little heart was beating triple time. He clutched her so hard she didn't think the skin on her shoulder beneath her blouse would ever be the same.

"Sorry," the photographer muttered, looking helpless.

By now everyone in the store assumed she was abusing her child. "It's not your fault." She turned to Angie in panic. "I'm taking him home."

"As soon as I pay for Danice's picture, I'll see you back at the apartment."

Paula nodded.

"It's all right, sweetheart. It's all right," she murmured as she hurried down the aisle to the entrance with her screaming child. Once outside, she practically ran through the parking lot toward her car. She had some treats and a bottle in her baby bag.

Footsteps were gaining on her. "Paula? What can I do to help?"

Her heart gave a loud thump. Walker? What were the chances of him showing up in time for another crisis with Clay?

"If you would open the passenger door for me, I'll let him sit with me for a minute until I can get him calmed down."

As soon as she sat with her jean-clad legs still outside the car, Walker hunkered down in front of her and removed the gold chain from his neck. Without saying a word to Clay, he swung the jade piece back and forth until he captured her son's attention.

In another minute the tears stopped gushing down his blotchy red cheeks. It was like a miracle. His breath caught several times and pretty soon his little hand let go of her upper arm and he reached for it.

"You like that?" The second Walker asked the question in a velvety voice, Clay put it to his mouth and bit on it. A deep chuckle rose from Walker's throat. It resonated to every cell of Paula's body.

She looked at him in awe. "I'm impressed."

His sober gaze flicked to hers. "I don't know much about children, but I've been around horses all my life. When something frightens them, the only thing you can do is distract them until they forget why they're nervous."

She bit her lip. "I took him in to get his photograph taken, but he wouldn't look at the camera, so the man—"

"I saw the whole thing," Walker interrupted her quietly. "I happened to be at the camera counter picking up some special pictures I had made up for my mother. When he brought out the bear, I was afraid Clay might associate it with the black Lab."

Paula blinked. "Of course—"

"It reminded me of the first time my father made me sit on the back of a horse. I was probably Clay's age. It was huge to me. Unpredictable. It took me years to get over my fear of horses, but I had to hide my terror in front of my father because he wouldn't tolerate cowardice."

"Walker—" Her throat had almost closed from the emotions that had been building. "To think you ended up becoming a champion steer wrestler."

"Yup." He stared at her. "It boggles the mind, especially since I saw myself in Clay just now. Sure enough, he took one look at the bear and terror caused him to burst into tears."

His gaze slid back to Clay's. He tousled his blond curls. To her surprise a sweet smile broke out on her son's face, softening the look in Walker's eyes. "You're just like me, aren't you, sport? You have to be gentled first."

Without knowing it, Walker had just handed her a key to his very complex soul. "Thanks again for your help," she whispered. After the way their phone conversation had ended the other night, she couldn't have imagined a moment like this.

"You're welcome." The second he stood up and kissed Clay's forehead, she knew he was going to leave. "Be a good boy for your mother."

"Just a minute and I'll give you back the jade, but first I have to convince Clay to let me have it."

"I'm afraid I don't have time. As it is I'm going to be late meeting up with my brother. Let him keep it. Maybe it will bring him luck."

Meaning what? That the jade piece hadn't worked for Walker after all? Was there a tinge of despair she'd heard in his voice? He walked away. Twice now he'd said goodbye to her and meant it. She got it.

But while she moved to put Clay in his car seat, she was aware of an inexplicable sense of loss. In spite of her determination to put Walker in her dead-end file, feelings for him insisted on growing beneath her surface attraction to him. They grew stronger as she watched his truck pull out of the parking lot onto the highway and disappear.

Chapter Five

May 12

Good old reliable Jesse was waiting for Walker when he pulled up in the parking area at the side of the new ranch house Wednesday evening. They'd dressed alike in jeans and checked, long-sleeved shirts; Jesse's in brown-and-white, Walker's in blue-and-white. He was still breaking in his new cowboy boots, but he'd left the hat at home.

The family would have to stare at their underweight prodigal son with his Marine cut. Though he'd put on five pounds since getting out of the hospital, and his hair was getting longer, he by no means resembled the man who'd left home six years ago. That man with the overly long black hair had needed a sturdier horse to carry his weight.

Jesse walked over to him as he climbed down from the cab. "You look a damn sight better than you did at the motel." They hugged. "Mom's been biting her nails that you might not show."

That was a joke between them because their mother had never done such a thing and never would, but they could always tell how nervous she was if she started humming off-key while she worked.

"So she's been humming up a storm?"

"Yup, and it's driven everyone crazy."

Walker laughed. He couldn't help it. Jesse was like a dose of something savory after a steady diet of the inedible.

"Walk around the back of the house with me. Elly and the twins are in the pool. Mom's in the kitchen. She set up a barbecue on the deck. Steaks, ribs. The works."

"Nice." It was a warm, beautiful night for it. "Where's Dad?"

Jesse's brows lifted. "Probably upstairs getting showered and dressed, and nervous as hell."

"Don't you mean angry?"

His brother had no answer for that. Walker couldn't wait to get this reunion over with. As they made the tour around back, his hand went to his throat before he realized the jade piece was no longer resting against his chest beneath the shirt. He felt naked and vulnerable without it. In truth he longed to feel the touch of Paula's hands on his skin one more time as she fastened it around his neck....

"Walker!"

Elly squealed in delight the second she saw him and launched herself out of the pool wearing a bright red bikini. He could see right away his tallish sister was no longer a tomboy. With her blond hair braided on top of her head, she'd turned into a real beauty.

He hurried across the deck and swung her around before giving her a hug.

"Elly...you're a sight for sore eyes."

Hers, a mixture of green and blue, were tear-filled as she examined him. "So are you. I'm so glad you're home," she cried in a broken voice and wrapped her arms around his chest again. "Sorry I'm getting you wet."

"Do you think I care?"

"I prayed for you every night."

"I heard them," he said for her ears alone.

"Hey, you guys. Is this a private club or what?"

"Dusty…" Walker swung around to embrace his brother, who looked like an improved version of Brad Pitt. "How are the ladies treating you these days?" With that dimple of his, he'd always been dynamite with the opposite sex.

"I'm not complaining." His blue eyes danced as they teased. "It's a good thing you're finally home so we can put some meat on your bones. It's been a long time."

"Too long," Walker admitted, finding it difficult to swallow because of the emotions tearing him up one side and down the other. He had no quarrel with his siblings. That's what was killing him.

Behind Dusty he could see Dex sitting at the edge of the pool waiting his turn. Being fraternal twins, they both had their own good looks and unique mannerisms. Dex had always been the quiet one. Walker reached down and gave him a hand to pull him up. His dark blond brother responded with a bone-crushing squeeze. He wasn't a team roper for nothing. When he let go, more scrutiny took place.

"Is that another scar under your chin?" Walker asked.

Dex grinned. "It's the same one from before, but it's a little raw from getting dragged around the practice arena the other day. You look taller, you know that? If that's what the Marines do for you, maybe I'll join. I always wanted a few more inches like you."

Whatever Walker might have answered was lost when he heard, "Welcome home, son."

He braced himself before turning around. J.W. looked fit as he stood beneath the overhang of the deck in a tan Western shirt and jeans. There were more steel threads in his black hair, but all in all, he didn't seemed changed. From the distance between them he felt his father's glittering gaze.

Though Walker was the tallest in the family, his father had always appeared bigger than life to him. The cane only seemed to add to his aura of unquestioned authority.

His father didn't move toward him. It was up to Walker, who felt as though he was moving through quicksand to reach him. "You look like you're doing well. It's good to see you, Dad."

Walker meant it. It *was* good to see the man who'd given him life, who'd taught him everything he thought he should know, who'd provided a lifestyle for his children any son would thank God for.

J.W. didn't say anything, but Walker noticed the throb at his temple, denoting his tension. They shook hands, adding to the awkwardness he felt in front of his siblings, who'd gone so quiet it was unnatural. Did his father know that he knew his secret?

He'd seen his mother come out on the patio, but she paused when she saw what was happening and stood at a distance.

Hell—

"Mom says to come and get it," his older brother blurted from the banquet table laden with enough food for a small army. Jesse, Jesse. Once again, he'd ridden into the fort at the last moment bringing fresh troops.

Walker was first at the table. He hugged his mother and they talked for a minute, then he started piling the food on his plate. Everyone clamored cheerfully to be heard, and a good deal of bantering went on before they found deck chairs placed near each other.

Anything to do with rodeo standings proved the safest topic of conversation. He questioned each of them about their latest triumphs and defeats. They reminisced about past championships, including his. There was more talk about future competitions. His father weighed in on the subject of the new Corriente bulls trucked in from Mexico after being in quarantine.

Walker noticed they all stayed away from asking him questions about Iraq, no doubt Jesse's doing. His mother wanted to know if he was comfortable at the cabin. That prompted him to turn to Dex.

"If I come down to the practice arena one of these mornings, will you be there to help me get my feet wet again? I need to do it as part of my therapy."

His brother glanced at everyone in stunned surprise before he said, "You just name the day, Walker."

"That would be terrific. Thanks, Dex."

After a big serving of strawberry shortcake, one of Walker's favorite desserts, Elly said, "As soon as the food has digested, let's have a game of water polo. I want to see if Walker can still whomp everybody."

Unless the family was prepared to see his scars, Walker figured it wouldn't be a good idea. Jesse picked up on his anxiety. "Maybe later, Elly. In the meantime I'll show Walker the new horse barn. It's not that far from here. You're going to be impressed, bro."

"Let's go, then."

"I'll walk over there with you," their father said.

Walker sensed what was coming, but there wasn't anything he could do about it. He gave his mom a peck on the cheek, then started around the side of the house with Jesse and his dad.

Well out of earshot of the others, his father stopped midstride and looked over at him. "I'm glad to hear you want to get back on a horse again, son. The ranch could use your help. Ask Jesse and he'll tell you. Any time you say, you can be in charge of the bulls we're working with right now. Jesse will set you up. When you're settled in, you can start flying down to Mexico and take charge of that end of the operation."

"I know there isn't anything Jesse wouldn't do for me, but I'm not looking for a job. Right now I'm just trying to focus on getting better both mentally and physically." Of course until

Walker got on a horse and went through the motions, he didn't know if he had what it took to even compete anymore.

His father got that look on his face that meant he'd dug in his heels. "How long do you expect to go on like this?" he demanded. The lid was coming off.

"I wish I knew, but I don't."

"Well, you sure as hell better find out fast." Suddenly it was just the two of them. "What do you mean you don't know?" he asked.

"I'm at a crossroads trying to figure out my life."

J.W. frowned. "What's there to figure out? You're home with your family now. You could have your pick of any job on the ranch you want."

"That's the problem, Dad. I don't know what I want." He had one idea that had nothing to do with the horses or the cattle, but he wasn't about to discuss it with his father tonight.

"So what you're saying is, military life offered you more than anything the ranch could. If that's the case, how come you bothered to come home at all?" His withering tone caused Walker to struggle for breath.

"When I got injured, I couldn't go back into combat for a couple of months. While I was in the hospital, I decided to resign my commission."

His father's expression froze. "How come you didn't tell anybody?"

"I'm telling you now."

"So you're just going to stay up at the cabin and waste away out of sight? Is that it?"

"Not exactly. I'm doing rehab at the VA clinic in Powell trying to follow my doctor's advice."

"That's good."

"But it means I need a little time."

"Time be damned, son! I thought the Marines were

supposed to teach you how to be a man and take responsibility. To stay up on the mountain alone isn't normal and doesn't sound like any son of mine."

Nope. Walker had always been different from the others, and now his father was saying it.

"Are you on drugs?" He took hold of his arm. "That's the kind of weird you learn in the military I don't like."

"I'm not on anything."

"You'd better not be!"

"I assure you that's the last thing I'd want to do."

"Let's hope so. You're a Cody. You're supposed to be tough!" He let go of him and spread his hands wide. "I built this house so all my children could stay here if they want. Your room's ready and waiting for you. Move in here and we'll fatten you up."

"You're very generous, Dad. You always have been. Please don't think I'm not appreciative of all you and Mother do for me, but I've been on my own for years now.

"You can't honestly expect me to live with my parents."

"I didn't mean forever." By now his face had gone a ruddy color.

"I realize that."

The chasm kept widening. "Just don't you go disappointing me by drinking yourself to death or some such nonsense!"

"I don't drink or smoke, either. Doctor's orders."

His father cleared his throat. "I'm glad to hear it. You trust this doctor in Powell?"

"Yes. He's exceptional and knows what he's doing. I was at his support group last night."

J.W. scratched his head. "That's fine, but you've got a support group out there at the pool. The best one you could ever ask for."

"I know that. I love all of them."

"Then show it! Be with us. Get back to your old self! Your

mother puts up a good front, but for you to come home after all this time and still want to be alone is eating her alive."

He couldn't handle talk about hurting his mother, not after what his father had done to her. Walker's hand reached for the jade talisman like a lifeline, only to remember once again that he'd given it to Clay.

"Let's join the others." Without waiting for his dad's response, he walked around to the pool once more. Everyone had jumped back in except for Jesse.

"Come on in!" Elly called to him.

"Another time."

"Ah, come on!" Dusty kept it up.

"I would, but I've had some surgery and it's not a pretty sight."

"Likely excuse," Dex teased.

Walker looked around. His parents had gone in the house. This might be the best time to show them so they wouldn't think he was being deliberately aloof. "Jesse's already seen my mark of bravery. Since you guys already know what a bull can do to us in the arena, this shouldn't be anything new."

He turned to the side and pulled the shirt out of his waistband, lifting it up so they could see the part of his anatomy that was scarred. "It goes down my hip. There were three of us that got hit with an IED. I was the lucky one who came home."

A collective gasp came from his siblings. It was called shock therapy for your loved ones. This peep show was enough for tonight. They didn't want to know what was going on inside of him....

EARLY THURSDAY MORNING, Paula dressed in jeans and a straw-colored sweater before heading out to the Cottonwood Ranch. As she drove up to the side of the Cody ranch house she noticed there were a couple of trucks in the parking area.

She'd brought Clay with her. While she worked, she would push him along in his stroller. He was especially good-natured in the morning, which was the best time for her to walk around and do a few quick sketches.

She wanted to be here as the light peered over the mountain. That way she could see where the rays illuminated several gentle slopes she had in mind for the gardeners to plant bulbs of yellow tulips and white daffodils with yellow centers. More yellows were needed among the plantings on the east side. If she found the right spot, it would look as if golden flowers had just spilled from the sun.

After finishing one drawing, she moved on to the west side of the ranch house, where she worked up a sketch for splashes of purple, burgundy and pink tulips planted together to provide a foil for the greenery. When the sun's rays slanted on that part of the grounds, the explosion of colors would remain in the beholder's mind long after the sun had fallen below the horizon.

An hour later, after she'd filled in the sketches with quick-drying acrylics to bring colorful life to the paper, she phoned Walker's mother as prearranged and asked her to meet her outside.

Once upon a time, Paula had thought of her as Anne Cody, but no longer. The trim woman in Western clothing walking toward her like a young girl had given birth to five children, but in Paula's mind none were as remarkable as her second-born son.

No matter how hard she tried, Paula couldn't rout him from her consciousness the way you might remove the intrusive day lily from a carefully tended garden. His roots had sunk deep in her psyche and were there to stay.

"Good morning, you two!" Anne walked right over to

Clay, who was playing with a puzzle toy in his stroller. She gave him a kiss. "I swear he gets bigger every time I see him."

"He's heavier, too," Paula said wryly. "How are you, Anne? You're looking well."

Her keen blue glance darted to Paula. "I can't complain."

No, but the older woman wasn't jumping for joy, either. The artist in Paula detected a trace of sorrow in the lines around her eyes and mouth.

Every family had its problems. As Paula's mother used to say, at any given moment she was only as happy as her saddest child. Maybe that's what was wrong with Anne Cody, who knew her son had been suffering since his return from war. Much as she wanted to talk to her about Walker, she didn't dare.

Keepings things to business, Paula handed her the sketch pad. "Take a look and tell me what you think."

Anne lifted the cover. "Oh, Paula…" she cried.

The satisfying reaction was all she could ask for. "That's a grouping of Queen of the Night, Burgundy Lace and Greenland tulips." She pointed out the area where she envisioned them planted.

"It surpasses anything I had imagined."

Paula smiled. "I'm glad. Now take a look at the next page. The flowers will be planted on the slopes at the east side of the house. Here you see the Golden Apeldoorn Darwin tulips planted with Golden Echo daffodils. The spots of color are California poppies. I've written all the names down for your gardener."

"This is really fabulous, Paula."

"I'm glad you like them. I'll leave both drawings with you to show your husband and the gardener. You might want to add more colors and can talk it over with them." She removed the pages from her sketchbook.

Anne lifted her gaze to Paula. "Everyone who comes here raves about the landscaping. When these flowers bloom next spring, they'll bring crowds of people. I'm thrilled to death over what you've designed."

"If this is what you had pictured in your mind, then I'm pleased. Now I'd better get going. Clay has been remarkably good this morning, but now it's time to go home for a diaper change and a snack."

"Won't you come in the house? Barbara will make him something."

"Another time and I'd love to, but I have to get back to work on a project waiting for me."

"I understand. I've got work myself."

They walked as far as the front entrance. Before Anne went back in the house she paused. "My son Walker isn't one to comment about anything unless he means it, so I have to tell you something he said to me at our family party last night."

Paula's pulse rate picked up just to hear his name mentioned. She was glad he'd been with them.

"He told me the food's perfect and so is the landscaping."

Those words meant a lot coming from his mother. "That's nice to hear. I'll always be grateful for his quick reflexes at the dog parade. Your son is a remarkable man."

Anne's eyes grew cloudy. "I hope one day he begins to believe it." She cleared her throat. "Thank you for coming out here this morning. My husband says you can do no wrong. Wait until he sees these!" She gave Paula a hug and went inside the house.

A little giddy that Walker had praised her work, Paula

pushed the stroller around the house to the parking area. She opened the rear passenger door. "In you go, sweetheart."

As she started to fasten Clay in his car seat, a truck pulled up next to her. Her heart thudded in her chest to see it was a black truck.

She groaned.

Walker shot her an indefinable glance before levering himself from the cab with consummate male grace. He wore a long-sleeved hunter-green shirt and Levi's tucked into his cowboy boots. She had to admit his looks were even more compelling when he needed a shave.

Before either of them spoke, Clay made excited sounds that drew their attention. As Walker moved closer, her son extended his hands and tried to get out of his car seat to reach Walker.

"Hey, sport." A smile broke out on Walker's face, transforming him into someone impossibly handsome. "I'm happy to see you, too." He glanced at Paula. "Do you mind if I hold him?"

Tongue-tied, she gestured that it was okay. Then, as if it were the most natural thing in the world, he undid the restraint and pulled Clay out of the car seat. Her son hugged him in obvious delight. Incredible. Paula watched Walker carry Clay around while he talked to him.

"It looks like you're all over your fright of the other day." He stopped in front of Paula, sending her a frank stare. "Did he have any nightmares after the incident with the bear?"

"No. He's been fine."

"That's good." He cocked his dark head. "I take it you've been out here working already this morning."

"Yes."

"With my mother?"

"Yes." Good grief… Couldn't she talk in more than

monosyllables? "A-are you feeling more settled in?" she stammered.

"Do you mean, am I getting back to my old routine? I guess I am. Later today I'm leaving for California."

"You're taking a trip?"

"Not exactly. I'm flying down to the rodeo in Redding for the weekend with the family."

Her head lifted. "Does this mean you're only supplying moral support, or are you returning to the rodeo yourself?"

"Both. Of course the latter depends on my not being over the hill."

"Don't be absurd," she bit out before she could recall the words. "After the way you handled yourself at the dog parade, I'd say you haven't lost any of your speed."

"Thanks for the vote of confidence," came his mocking reply.

"You're welcome."

The tension between them was explosive. "So are you a fan of steer wrestling?" he asked.

"I've only been to one rodeo in my life. That must have been when I was about twelve. My brother's a different story however. Kip and his best friend used to enter local bulldogging events and both have the mended broken bones to prove it."

His green eyes kindled with interest. "Where was this?"

"In Idaho."

"You're not from Wyoming, then?"

"No. I was brought up on a ranch outside Rexburg."

"What kind?"

"A small one. Compared to the Cottonwood Ranch, it's miniscule. Dad grows barley, sugar beets and alfalfa. Kip's in business with him."

"Is he married?"

"No. As he continues to tell my parents, he's only twenty-seven and has years yet."

Walker's lips twitched. Her heart turned over when he looked like that. "Do you ride when you go home for visits?"

"Yes. Dad has a mare called Trixie. I usually take her out for exercise. Kip has his own quarter horse, Lefty. He always had a dream to compete in the pro rodeo circuit as a steer wrestler, but he wasn't good enough. Certainly nothing like you."

He slanted her a glance. "That means my father was talking out of school again. I'm afraid he has a one-track mind when it comes to the rodeo. I'm sorry you had to be a captive audience while you worked with him."

"I found it fascinating. Your parents told me you won the world steer-wrestling championship seven years ago. The other day while I was talking to Kip on the phone and told him I'd met you, he almost had a heart attack. I didn't know it, but he mounted a bunch of posters in the barn and you're on one of them."

Walker scoffed. "The barn's where those posters belong."

She sucked in her breath. "Is it true what I heard about your best friend?"

He looked away. "Afraid so. While he was in the box, his horse reared for some reason. It threw his head against the bar, and he suffered a fatal concussion."

A shudder rocked her body. "That's horrible. What was his name?"

"Troy Pearsoll. It happened at the Cody Roundup."

A long silence ensued before she said, "How long ago did he die?"

"It's been six years."

She swallowed hard. "Is that why you became a Marine?"

"If that's what my father told you, he's wrong."

His withering delivery stopped her cold. So did his news about getting back into competition. According to Kip, the steers used on the national pro circuit raised the bar of danger to another level altogether.

Wishing she hadn't asked so many questions, she averted her eyes and went around to stash the stroller and other things in the trunk. "If you wouldn't mind putting Clay in the car seat, I need to get home and back to work."

"Did you hear that?" He spoke to Clay as he fastened him inside. "Your mommy says you have to leave. Be a good boy for her, sport." With another kiss to Clay's temple, he shut the door.

"Walker," she called out at the last second, "if I'd known we would happen to see each other here, I would have brought your jade piece with me."

"Don't worry about it."

She wished she didn't. She wished she could erase him from her consciousness, but was finding it impossible. Now to learn he was getting back to a dangerous sport that had killed his best friend, her concern for him had just been raised another dozen notches. At this point he was going to need more than luck.

"All you have to do is come by the apartment on your way to or from therapy one of these days. Give me a call first and I'll leave the jade out on top of the milk box for you."

His expression remained inscrutable before he gave her a nod that meant he'd heard what she'd said, but he made no verbal commitment. Leaving her at a loss, he strode around the house until he was out of sight. No doubt he'd come to visit his parents.

Paula started her car and drove out to the main road leading to the Cottonwood Ranch entrance. By the time she passed beneath the antler arch, she had to accept the fact that she'd come down with a bad case of what she could only describe as *pervasive walkeritis*. There didn't appear to be any known cure.

ALL YOU HAVE TO DO is come by the apartment on your way to or from therapy.

Was that code to mean Paula wanted to see him again?

His lips thinned. Hell no. Not if she planned to leave his gift on the milk box! Once a widow, always a widow. If that was the message she'd intended to send him, he'd received it in spades!

In a foul mood, Walker hurried inside to find his mother. She'd begged him to give her his packet of pictures from Iraq for a scrapbook she was making. While he was here, he decided to get the boxes from his room that held his college books and papers.

Little did he realize that in coming here, he'd see Paula again. It sent every thought out of his head but one. He'd been trying to stay away from her, but they just kept bumping into each other. *Got any strategies for that, Dr. Bader?*

After a short chat with his mother, who showed him Paula's drawings for her bulb gardens, he hunted down the two boxes he needed and loaded them in the backseat of the truck. With that accomplished, he left to join his brothers.

Paula filled his thoughts as he maneuvered the truck past the round and square pens. Morning or night, she was a knockout. Everything about her appealed to him. Why was he hung up on her when he knew he was poison to her? He needed his brain rewired.

His teeth grated all the way to the open-air arena where he climbed out of the cab. In the distance he spotted a bunch of hands assembled while Dex and Dusty, mounted on their horses, were waiting for a steer to leap out of one of the chutes.

Of the two, Dusty had always had the most talent in the team roping and was the header, but Dex, the heeler, displayed beauty of motion on a horse.

Walker watched in anticipation, waiting for the steer to be released, but the second it leaped out of the chute he could see its hind legs wouldn't hop.

Dusty rode out on a big bay. He stayed to the left of the steer and threw a graceful loop around the horns, but Dex reined in his chestnut, not bothering to tie up the feet. "That's the second dragger in this new bunch," he muttered in disgust, resettling his cowboy hat in frustration. "Dad's not going to be happy about this latest shipment of steers."

"Better tell him today," Dusty said before he saw Walker leap over the barrier and approach them in a few swift strides. "I don't believe it!" he cried.

By now Dex had seen him and broke into a broad smile. "Hey, bro." The twins dismounted and met him halfway while a couple of hands chased the steer out and took care of their horses. "What in the heck? We didn't expect to see you down here until after we got home from Redding!"

He sucked in his breath, still feeling the aftereffects of Paula Olsen. "Didn't Jesse tell you I'm flying down with you? In the meantime I've decided to start practicing for the Cody Roundup on the Fourth of July and thought I'd pick out the right dogie this morning."

They looked at each other, then tossed their hats in the air and let go with an ear-piercing "Woo-eee!" Everyone on the ranch had to have heard it.

Walker couldn't help but chuckle. Deep inside it touched him that they acted so happy about it. "You won't be whooping it up when you see what a disaster I'm going to be. People will say twenty-eight's too old for a bulldogger and boo me out of the arena."

"Just let 'em try." Dusty's fighting words meant something. He didn't get his wild reputation for nothing.

Dex nodded. "You can practice here or at the new arena every day. We'll help you whether we're in or out of town."

"You still want Boyd Summerhays to be your hazer?" Dusty asked. "You were always his idol. Just say the word and I'll arrange it today."

The twins were amazing. His father had spoken the truth when he'd told Walker all the support group he needed was right here in his own family.

"Your confidence in me is very gratifying. I'd love all the help you can give me."

Dex picked up his hat and brushed it off. "Let's take a look at the horses right now. I have a seven-year-old in mind that's fast on the takeoff and will handle your weight."

"You're thinking Peaches?" Dusty asked as the three of them left the arena and walked over to the barn. The familiar smell brought back a flood of memories so powerful, Walker was staggered by them.

"Yup. He's our sturdiest quarter horse."

"I've gained five pounds and am still trying to put on the rest."

"By the time July rolls around, you'll be there," Dex assured him. They walked past several stalls. "Here he is."

Walker moved inside and smoothed his hand down the animal's back. He was impressed that the dun-colored gelding didn't act spooked by a stranger. A calm temperament was everything in the ring.

"Peaches is fifteen hands. Just right for leaning out of the saddle."

He could see that. "You want to be my new buddy?" he whispered to the horse while he rubbed his soft nose. "It's been six years for me. I'm going to need your help now that I'm an old man."

His brothers laughed. "That'll be the day," Dex said with genuine affection. "You want Paco to saddle him up for you right now?"

"Thanks, but I'll do the honors. Peaches and I need to get acquainted if we're going to do this thing right."

Dusty studied him for a moment. "Your lucky saddle's still waiting for you in the tack room in its place of honor."

Walker's eyes smarted. Like old times, his brothers followed him on back. As he reached for his bridle and saddle, emotions threatened to swallow him alive. When he'd left the ranch to go into the Marines, he'd thought he was hanging up everything for good, vowing it was the end for him.

But that's what he got for thinking, because he needed a way to deal with a whole host of problems and had a hunch bulldogging might just be his salvation. Walker carried everything back to the stall. The weight felt familiar in his arms. He inhaled the smell of the leather.

How many times had he saddled up his horses since he was a child? Thousands? Did you ever really take the cowboy out of the boy? He'd thought he could....

In a few minutes he led Peaches out of the barn by the reins and walked him to the arena. After going on foot several times so the horse would get used to him, he finally levered himself into the saddle. The action was as natural as it was exhilarating. When he'd been in the hospital at the lowest ebb of his life, debating whether he could face going home, he couldn't have imagined this day.

Peaches seemed to accommodate him without problem. While he put the horse through his paces, an audience had gathered without his knowledge. When they broke into spontaneous applause, he lifted his head to see what was going on and noticed his brothers with a half-dozen hands cheering him.

He galloped over to them. "You guys know how to make an old vet feel like he's not completely washed up."

"You look good up there, Walker," Big Ben shouted with a smile on his face.

The second in command at the ranch had been there a good twenty years. "Welcome back."

"Amen," the twins echoed. Their blue eyes looked suspiciously bright.

The experience was a humbling one. "Thanks, everybody. It's good to be home." Like the Grinch at Christmas, he could feel his heart growing. He sent Dusty a glance. "If you want to ask Boyd to meet me here before we fly out, I'd like to talk to him."

"You've got it."

"When you went in the Marines, he worked with other partners, but it was never the same for him. Wait till he hears from Dusty. He'll think he's won the lottery again!" Dex blurted.

Auburn-haired Boyd, three years younger, had been his hazer when he'd won the world championship. He'd worked with him right up to the night Walker knew he had to get away from his father or lose it.

"We'll see." Walker eyed his brothers. "I've interrupted your practice time long enough. Remember you're competing tonight so don't break any legs out here this morning," he teased before heading to the barn. After removing the bridle and saddle, he watered Peaches and curried him.

The twins knew their horseflesh. "You're going to do fine." He gave the quarter horse a friendly pat and some oats before leaving. After lunch he'd load Peaches in one of the horse trailers and drive to the rangeland beyond the wells. They'd get better acquainted while they rode around the property. He did his best thinking on the back of a horse.

There was just one problem. All roads seemed to lead to Paula Olsen. What in the hell was he going to do about her?

Chapter Six

May 16

Sunday afternoon, Paula's cell rang while she was helping Clay to feed himself spaghetti. More got on the floor and the tray of his high chair than went in his stomach.

She wiped her hands with a paper towel before answering her phone. Anyone else could be calling, but not Walker. After Thursday she knew she wouldn't be seeing him unless it was because of another accidental meeting. Since the dog parade they'd been the proverbial ships passing in the night, both bound for different destinations—their courses set.

But she hadn't counted on her life seeming bleak in a brand-new way.

Since Brent's death she'd been functioning well enough because Clay gave her a reason to get up in the morning. He was her whole life now. Yet thoughts of Walker kept intruding, disturbing her equilibrium. It made no sense.

"Hello?"

"Paula?"

"Hi, Kip!"

"Are you still in Garland with your in-laws?"

"No. I came home last night."

"That's good. Have you heard the news?" he asked in a serious tone.

"What news? What are you talking about?"

He made a sound in his throat. "You need to check out the video posted on Rodeo Pro."

She got a suffocating feeling in her chest and gripped her phone tighter. "Why?"

"Walker Cody's sister got hurt barrel racing last night."

Paula lurched in her chair, thankful it wasn't Walker, but was worried sick for his sister and their family. "How serious was it?"

"I don't know. There's nothing on the regular news. I thought maybe you would know since you've been seeing Walker."

"I haven't been seeing him the way you mean, Kip."

"Sorry if I touched a nerve." Her eyes closed for a moment because she knew she was being supersensitive about Walker. "Are you by your computer?"

"No. I'm feeding Clay his lunch, but I'll go in the other room."

She rolled his high chair to the doorway between the kitchen and dining room so she could keep an eye on him. After sitting down, she put on the speakerphone, then typed in the Web address. Up popped the page with the video.

"Have you found it yet?"

"Yes. I'm starting it now."

"Get ready for this, folks. Elly Cody from Markton, Wyoming, her dad, J.W., and brothers, all of them here, even the legendary Walker Cody, back from the Marines after being gone the last few years. Every one of them is a champion in every arena they've ever nodded their head in.

"Elly has started hot and needs to keep going now around the third barrel. That's the fastest time of the barrel racers. Woo-eee! Her star just keeps ris— Uh-oh. Something's gone wrong. She's off her horse. She—"

The video ended too soon.

Paula groaned. "The poor thing. I'm going to call the ranch and see if I can reach Anne." She had no idea where Walker might be and didn't have his cell-phone number.

"Let me know what you find out."

"I will. Thanks for telling me, Kip."

"Sure."

She looked up the Codys' number from the client list she kept on her cell phone and punched in the numbers.

On the second ring, someone picked up. "John Walker Cody residence."

Paula recognized the housekeeper's voice. "Hello, Barbara? This is Paula Olsen."

"How are you, Mrs. Olsen?"

"I'm well, but I'm concerned about Elly Cody. I heard she'd been hurt at the rodeo in Redding. Is she all right?"

"Just a minute. I'll put one of her brothers on. Everyone's here."

Perspiration beaded her forehead before Walker's deep voice came over the line. "Paula?"

It was hard to swallow. "Walker? My brother just phoned me and told me about the accident. I saw it on a video." Her voice shook. "Is Elly—"

"She's fine," he broke in. "At first they thought she might have a spine injury, so they took her out on a board with a neck brace. But it turned out she was only stunned. There's nothing broken. Only a scratch on her elbow. She's here at the house taking it easy. More than anything she's just shaken up."

"I'm thankful for that."

"Me, too."

"What went wrong?"

"For some reason the horse she was riding got disoriented by the light and ran into a half-closed gate, knocking her out of the saddle. But she's tough and plans to compete next weekend in Hugo, Oklahoma, on her favorite horse."

She bowed her head. "I'm so relieved."

"We all are."

"I've never met her, but your parents have talked about her. Please give her my best wishes."

"I will." There was a distinct pause. "After her accident I decided I want my lucky charm back. How about I treat you to a picnic tomorrow in exchange for it? For part of the day anyway. That is if you can arrange some time off from work."

A picnic? While all the warning bells were going off in her head she said, "That sounds like a fair trade. Can we do it earlier rather than later in the day?"

"I'll be by at nine for you and Clay."

A FEW HOUSEKEEPING DUTIES and Walker was ready for his guests. On the way to Paula's apartment he stopped for more groceries and filled up the truck's gas tank.

At five to nine he pulled in front of the fourplex and got out.

"Hi!" Paula called to him from the railing outside her apartment. She carried Clay in her arms. "I'm almost ready."

"There's no hurry." Her compassion had prompted her to phone the house yesterday asking about Elly. In so doing she'd stepped over an imaginary line into his territory.

Though his instincts had warned him against any more contact with a woman still in love with her dead husband, he'd seized the moment anyway. Maybe a full dose of Brent Olsen being with them today would provide the wake-up call Walker needed to stay away for good.

"While I gather up the rest of the things, would you mind getting in my Toyota and removing the car seat? You'll have to take out the base, too." She used the remote on her keys to open the doors.

Walker nodded and glanced at the car seat. If he could wire munitions to blow up buildings and bridges, he ought to be able to handle a little kid's car seat, but this was going to be a first.

He had little problem extricating the car seat, but fitting the base into the backseat of his truck proved to be a challenge. After four tries, he figured it out. Just in time, too.

"Look, Clay. We're going to go for a ride in this great big truck. You love trucks."

Walker turned around in time to stare into eyes the color of blue pansies. In white cargo pants and a flowered top of apricot-and-white, she looked like a delicious summer treat. He tore his eyes from hers to look at Clay, who was busy playing with a toy car.

His eyes were a couple of shades lighter than his mother's. He was a good-looking mixture of both parents. She'd dressed him in denim shorts and a shirt with a cowboy logo. On his feet were the tiniest cowboy boots he'd ever seen. The sight made him chuckle. "I didn't know they came this small."

Her gentle laugh appealed to him. "My parents bought them. Dad can't wait until Clay can tromp around the ranch with him."

Unable to resist, Walker played with one of the toes to get Clay's attention. He swung his blond head around. When he saw who it was, he dropped the toy to reach for him.

"Hey, sport." He pulled him into his arms to hug him for a moment. Clay's eagerness to be with him caught him by surprise and warmed his heart. After he'd strapped him in the car seat, he told Paula he'd bring down the things she needed.

"If you'll carry the fold-up playpen and swing, I'll get

everything else. I know it's a lot of paraphernalia, but it'll be a blessing, believe me."

Laughing, he took the stairs two at a time and brought down the items in question. She moved past him to get the bags and lock the door. Soon they had everything stowed in the back and could take off.

In the quiet that followed, she looked over her shoulder at Clay. "This is a whole new experience for you, isn't it, sweetheart?"

"Is he always this good?"

"Generally speaking, yes, but you probably wouldn't believe it after the past two times we've been together. His is a sweet nature. In many ways he's like Brent."

Bingo.

There was nothing sweet about Walker. He grimaced. "Paula, there's something I need to tell you. In fact I should have brought it up before we left the apartment."

"What is it?"

"Sometimes I get flashbacks. If I'm around people when it happens, it's hard for me and I might act strange. It can be frightening because it comes out of the blue."

"You mean like the one you had that day at the dog parade?"

Her perception astonished him. "Yes."

"I didn't know it until just this minute. Now it makes sense that you thrust Clay in my arms and fled without a backward glance."

"I was afraid he would get injured if I didn't act immediately. Unfortunately the situation transported me back to Iraq. For a few minutes I got disoriented, just like the horse Elly was riding."

"No one would have known it. What you did was a brave act." Her voice throbbed. She glanced at him. "Do you get them often?"

"I had three in the hospital."

"Hospital? How badly were you injured?"

"I took a hit to my hip and the right side of my chest from an exploding IED. I was at Bethesda Naval Hospital for two months getting patched up. Since I've been back at the ranch, I've had two episodes—the one at the dog parade, and one the other night during the thunderstorm. But there'll be more. If you'd rather not be with me, I'll understand and take you home."

"I'm not frightened, Walker. Brent wouldn't talk to me about the war and what it did to him. With you, I feel like I'm finally getting a glimpse into what it means to be a soldier. He kept trying to shield me, but the more he refused to share it with me, the more I felt shut out.

"If you want to know the truth, there were times I was so angry after I'd gotten an e-mail from him that didn't tell me anything, I thought I'd explode. Because of it, I'm afraid some of my e-mails back didn't give him the comfort he needed."

She buried her face in her hands. "I've suffered a lot of guilt for not being the kind of wife he needed. Isn't that awful? When he died, it was too late to apologize to him."

He heard her grief and looked over at her. "If I'd left a wife and child like you and Cody at home, I probably wouldn't have shared that much with you, either."

Paula lifted her head, blinking back the tears. "I would rather have known the truth than be left thinking up horror stories that still percolate in my imagination."

"I'm afraid when Sherman said 'War is hell,' he didn't realize he was speaking for the spouses at home, too."

"If that's supposed to make me feel better, it doesn't." But she said it with a wry smile.

"Now that we have that settled, I'm surprised you haven't told me to turn the truck around."

"Only if you want to."

No. He didn't want to. He wanted her company. She was no fragile creature. He liked that. Not everyone possessed her gut-deep honesty, a trait that appealed to him more than a little bit.

THE MEADOW SURROUNDING the cabin was an explosion of scarlet red from all the wildflowers. With the mountain up close and knifing into the rarified atmosphere, Paula couldn't contain her ecstasy. She turned around, trying to take it all in. "What a stunning spot! I'd live up here every second if I could." It was the closest place to heaven she'd ever seen.

Walker had started unloading the truck. "My first memories of life began up here. This was my fort, my cave, my secret island. I was the king of my castle, lord of all I surveyed."

And now it was his refuge. But instead of saying the words, she pulled Clay from his car seat, nuzzling his neck to get out her emotions. "As soon as we go inside, I'll fix you a snack." Grabbing the baby bag, she headed for the charming cabin with spruce trees growing in the front yard.

Her host was there ahead of her to open the door. It opened into the kitchen with a big picture window on the right. With red print curtains and red linoleum to bring life to the honey-colored logs, it looked the way a small mountain cabin should look—cozy and inviting.

She put the bag on the picnic-table bench, then walked through to the living room. The fireplace was on the other side of the kitchen wall. Another picture window looked out on a different section of the meadow with blue flowers. There was a well-worn red print couch and two matching chairs on either side of it.

To the left, a staircase rose to the loft. Lots of family memorabilia covered the log wall. She couldn't wait to examine the photos. In the right corner a Dutch door led to a covered porch. Paula loved everything about the cabin, inside and out.

"Would you like me to set up the playpen in here or one of the bedrooms?"

She turned to him. "Since I'll only put him in it to sleep, maybe the bedroom would be best where it will be a little darker."

"What about the swing?"

"It makes a great high chair. I'll feed him in the kitchen, then we can take it anywhere. Come on, sweetie. I know you're hungry."

After setting it up, she lowered Clay into it and fastened the restraint. "There." She tied the bib around his neck. "Now what do you think?" She opened up the bag and pulled out his food. He jabbered away, eager for anything that tasted good.

Walker joined her on the bench as she was feeding Clay some cottage cheese. "What do you think he's saying?"

"Oh, lots of things. He loves the cabin and can't wait to climb up the stairs and pull down all those pictures, and then he wants to play with the knobs on those kitchen drawers."

Laughter broke out of Walker, the deep rich male kind she felt to her toes. What a wonderful sound when she thought he'd lost the capacity to laugh that way.

Like a little kid who couldn't contain his curiosity, he opened one of the plastic containers she'd brought. "Vienna sausages. I haven't had one of these in years."

"Take as many as you want. He'll only eat one or two."

To her delight, Walker ate three with obvious relish.

"Go ahead and feed him one."

He darted her a worried glance. "Will he take it from me?"

"There's only one way to find out."

When Walker lowered the sausage to his lips, Clay studied him for a moment and then opened his mouth and bit off the end so decisively, they both chuckled. When he'd swallowed that portion, he opened his mouth again. This time Walker pushed the sausage in farther, but it wouldn't go all the way.

"Kind of looks like Winston Churchill with his cigar, don't you think?" Paula quipped. By now Walker's shoulders were shaking with silent laughter. She pulled the little bit out. Clay took it from her fingers and stuffed it in his mouth. In another minute, all had been consumed.

"You see?" She turned her head to smile at Walker. "Feeding him is a piece of cake. You worried for nothing." His eyes, full of green flecks, smiled back. "Try giving him a banana." She'd pulled one out of the bag.

Walker reached for it and peeled it partway down. He leaned over. "You want some of this?" But when he put it near his mouth, Clay made another sound and brought his hand up to grab for it. In a lightning move he broke off the exposed part and shoved it in his mouth. This time Paula thought Walker would fall off the bench with laughter.

"This kid's tough."

"They're certainly not as fragile as they seem." Soon Walker had denuded the rest of the banana and was feeding Clay piece by piece. They were making excellent progress together. When he refused the last bite, Walker popped it in his own mouth.

"Looks like I'm going to have to wipe him down." Aware of Walker's gaze, she pulled some wipes out of the baby bag to clean off Clay's fingers and remove his bib. To keep her son busy, she handed him two of his favorite trucks.

While he was preoccupied, she reached inside the bag for the jade piece and put it on the table next to Walker. No way would she do the honors again.

His gaze fell to the charm. She held her breath until he'd fastened it around his neck. Relieved the moment had passed, she turned the dial that started the swing moving. "Now that Clay is enjoying himself, I meant to ask if you ever got started on your art therapy." When he'd invited her up here, he'd had an agenda and it wasn't to play house with her.

"There's plenty of time to talk about that. Why don't we take a walk outside first? There's a family of squirrels who live in the trees out in front."

Action. That's what she needed. Plenty of action and space. The kitchen suddenly seemed too small with both of them in it.

"Clay will love it!" She bent over the swing to undo the restraint and pull him out so he could walk.

Walker opened the door. "Come on, little guy." He grasped Clay's hand and paced himself to stay with him. Her son went right to him. She followed and closed the door before taking Clay's other hand.

It was like stepping into a carpet of flowers, reminding her of Dorothy in *The Wizard of Oz,* walking through the field of poppies set against an impossibly blue sky. There must have been some rain up here last night. Everything smelled so fresh. She detected an intoxicating scent in the air from the flowers.

For a little while Paula felt more alive than she'd been since before Brent had been deployed to Afghanistan.

While she was engrossed, Walker picked up Clay and moved a little closer to one of the trees where a couple of squirrels were running along the branches. Every so often they stopped and chattered. The fascinating sight held the three of them mesmerized. It wasn't just the animals enjoying their life undisturbed in this paradise. It was as if every element of nature had aligned in perfect harmony. She found it all so beautiful, it hurt.

Walker looked over at her. Their eyes met in an unsmiling glance that quickened her body because she knew he was feeling the magic of this moment, too. Paula was afraid to breathe for fear of disturbing the tranquility enveloping them. For a few minutes there was no war anywhere, no tragedy, no sorrow, only a precious window out of time they were privileged to share.

Suddenly the sound of a truck coming up the dirt road shattered the quiet. She hadn't seen it yet, but the squirrels didn't like the intrusion. They screeched and vanished into the highest branches of the tree. Clay squirmed in Walker's arms to see what was coming.

"Stay here." He handed Clay to her. "I'll see who it is," he muttered with a hardened jaw. In an instant he'd turned into the forbidding stranger she'd tried to talk to outside the movie theater in Cody.

He strode down the slope. She felt sorry for the person who'd decided to pay him an unexpected visit. From her own experience she'd learned you didn't approach Walker unless he wanted it. More fallout from the war, or had he always been an intensely private person?

Paula lowered Clay to the ground so he could walk around. She stayed with him while he stopped here and there to touch the flowers. Once or twice he rubbed his eyes, an indication he was getting ready for his nap.

Before long she spied a propane truck come up over the rise and drive around the back of the cabin. Then she saw Walker heading toward her. With every step that brought him closer, her heart thumped a little harder.

"Jesse didn't want me to run out of propane so he sent for the truck. It won't take them long."

"That was thoughtful of him."

"He takes care of everybody. One day he'll inherit the

ranch. Though he's known for his bull riding, no one will ever run the place better."

That was high praise coming from Walker. She heard real affection there. "While I was watching the video, the announcer said all the Codys were champions. I doubt there's another family like yours anywhere."

His expression closed up. "Not unless they have a father like mine."

After his comment about the monument J.W. had erected, she'd known he had issues with his father. This last statement just confirmed it.

"No, no, Clay!" She'd been so deep in thought, she hadn't realized her son was ready to put one of the paintbrush stalks in his mouth. "They might look good enough to eat, but they'll make you sick." Paula tossed the plant away before plucking him from the ground. "It's time for a little nap. Come on. Let's go in."

"What can I do to help?" Walker asked, after showing her the bedroom where he'd set up the playpen.

"If you'll bring in the baby bag, everything I need is in it."

"One baby bag coming up."

She laid Clay down on the double bed and took off his boots and socks. When Walker came back in, she reached inside the bag for the little plastic mat she used to change him. Once she'd pulled off his shorts, she whipped out a new diaper and put it under him before removing the old one. Walker watched in fascination as she fastened him up and put the used diaper in a Ziploc bag.

"There you go, sweetie." She pulled up his shorts before carrying him over to the playpen. He started to cry until she handed him his favorite blue blanket and a bottle she'd already filled with milk. "Time to go to sleep." He went quietly, looking up at the two of them while he made noisy sounds drinking his bottle.

Walker chuckled. "Listen to him guzzle that."

"He's hilarious."

"He's one lucky boy to have a mother like you."

Her face went warm. "Thank you, but he makes it easy."

As they tiptoed out of the room, she heard the truck start up and drive away from the cabin. Paula headed for the kitchen to wash her hands. Walker wasn't far behind.

"How do sloppy joes sound to you for lunch?"

"I love them."

"Good. I bought some corn on the cob, too."

"I don't suppose either item was included in your K rations."

He pulled the corn from a bag he'd brought in. "Not exactly. If you don't mind doing the shucking, I'll get the ground beef started."

They made desultory conversation while they put their meal together. It was a novel experience for Paula to be working alongside a man in the kitchen again. Within twenty minutes they sat down to one of the best meals she'd ever eaten. Of course the company had everything to do with her enjoyment.

Glad to see he had an appetite, she realized the gaunt look had disappeared from his face and he'd started to pick up a tan. She thought he'd even put on weight. All that was good, except that he looked tired. After Brent had been deployed, she'd read the literature on PTSD. Returning vets had trouble getting enough sleep. That plus the scare over his sister was causing his eyelids to droop.

When they'd done the dishes, she turned to him. "That meadow out the window is calling to me. Would you mind very much if I started a painting? Maybe you could take a little nap like Clay."

"Are you sure you wouldn't mind?" His question told her he liked the idea.

"Not at all. The scarlet of the paintbrush looks like flame. I'd like to capture it with the sun at this angle. It's been a long time since I was inspired." It was true. "Let's both take advantage of the quiet before my son wakes up."

"Maybe I'll lie down on the couch for a few minutes."

Five hours later Paula's mouth broke into a secret smile when she entered the cabin with Clay after their long walk and saw that Walker was still out for the count. He lay on his stomach with one arm dangling to the floor. His tall, lean body took up the couch from end to end.

He'd removed his cowboy boots. The comparison between them and Clay's tiny ones was amusing to say the least.

For Walker to be sacked out all afternoon meant he'd let go of that nervous energy for a while and could relax. To see him get this much relief from stress brightened her day in a way she couldn't put into words.

It was dinnertime. She didn't want to wake him until she had to. Once Clay ate some mac and cheese, she packed up the baby bag and art supplies and set them outside the cabin door.

Next she quietly loaded the swing and playpen and took them out to the truck. Clay walked along with her. On her return to the cabin she carried him in her arms. To her surprise, she was met by a fierce-looking Walker who'd come into the kitchen in his stocking feet.

He rubbed the back of his neck in what she perceived was abject frustration. "Why did you let me sleep all day?" His attractive voice sounded an octave lower.

"Because you obviously needed it. Please don't be upset. I've had one of the most relaxing days in years. This place is so beautiful I filled my sketch pad with drawings while Clay played by me.

"To be honest, ever since Brent left for Afghanistan, I haven't been able to paint, but being up here has unlocked something inside me. It was an unexpected gift. But now that you're up, I need to get Clay home. Do you mind?"

It was a lie, but she wasn't above using her son as the excuse to get away from Walker. Much more time spent here and she'd never want to leave. She heard him take a deep breath. "Of course not. Have you had anything to eat since lunch?"

"I snacked on and off all afternoon."

He didn't look as if he believed her. "Give me a minute and I'll meet you outside."

No sooner had she taken the other things to the truck and installed Clay in the car seat than Walker joined her in the cab. The tension he'd managed to let go of for part of the day seemed to be back in full force.

By the time they reached her apartment, she was glad to be home in the safety of familiar surroundings. While he brought her things in from the truck, she gave Clay a quick bath.

Once he was dressed in his jammies, she walked out to the living room with him. "Clay's ready for bed. Say nite-nite to Walker."

To her surprise, Clay leaped at the chance to be back in Walker's strong arms. He kissed his face the way he did with her. Then his hands found the chain and pulled the jade piece out of the neck of his T-shirt to bite it.

"No-no, sweetie. This isn't yours." She had to physically remove his fingers before he tugged too hard and broke the chain. Half laughing up at Walker, she said, "Now you know why I don't wear jewelry."

Paula had only recently removed her wedding rings and put them away. She planned to give them to Clay one day when he'd met the right girl, but that was years and years away yet.

Walker smiled. "Lead the way to the bedroom and I'll put him in bed."

"Let me get his bottle first."

To keep Brent alive in Clay's heart, she'd put different photos of his daddy around the nursery. Some pictured her with him. Others included the three of them. She saw Walker study each of them before he put Clay down and covered him with his blue blanket. She handed him his bottle. He played with it for a minute, then started to drink.

Paula left the room ahead of Walker and discovered a drawing pad with a set of pastels sitting on the coffee table. His, of course. Full of curiosity she reached for the pad and turned back the cover.

There were two pages with swirls of color. Mostly dark.

"What do you think?" came his deep voice.

"When did you do these?"

"A few days ago."

"What I think doesn't matter, Walker. I took a series of art classes in college. One of them covered the possible avenues to use an art degree. There was a section on art therapy. I actually considered it for a time, but I had a professor who talked me into going into landscape architecture. He said a lot of people needed help, but a lot of landscapes needed help, too."

That brought a quick white smile to Walker's lips. "He was right about that. As I told you before, the main ranch house would have been a disaster without the right surroundings."

Actually the Codys' new home was gorgeous—modern, yet its interior was all Western and decorated in superb taste. She suspected that Walker's dislike of it had more to do with his personal hang-ups.

She studied his drawing again. "I take it you're not thrilled about getting your emotions out through art."

"I wouldn't know how to begin."

"You got a good start here."

"I'm supposed to draw when I feel upset or restless."

"So far you've said quite a bit. Black with purple on one spectrum, yellow on the other. Hell and illumination. Two polar opposites. When you go back to the cabin tonight, suppose you do another drawing that expresses how you felt while you were in the hospital recovering from that IED.

"But before you leave, I'm going to give you my set of pastels. Just a minute and I'll get them." She came back from the dining room with her case. "The pack of eight he started you out with doesn't offer you the range of colors you need. He probably didn't want to overwhelm you on your first visit.

"Remember your emotions are as varied as the colors. There are seventy-five colors in my case. If you see the right one, it could put you in touch with how you were feeling. Then you just start scribbling like mad, the way you did as a child who draws from emotion. You may find yourself scribbling on many pages."

His eyes searched hers. "How did you get to be so wise?"

She let out a mirthless laugh. "You've asked the wrong person. I'm not dealing with my loss very well. Except for this afternoon, I haven't been able to put anything on paper except for my clients. *You* at least produced a glimpse of your inner self for the doctor. That took incredible courage. Looking inward is a frightening experience, one I haven't found the guts to try yet."

Walker wore a solemn expression as he gathered up his things. "My next group-therapy session is next Tuesday at seven. We're encouraged to bring family members and friends. If you'd like to come with me, it will give you a chance to talk to other vets and possibly get answers as to why Brent held back from you.

"My thinking is, you'll find he wasn't the only husband who couldn't open up. Hopefully with more understanding, it will help rid you of some of your guilt for being angry with him. Think about it. I'll give you a call when I'm ready to leave for Powell. If you decide to come, I'll swing by for you."

Chapter Seven

May 25

Walker surveyed the assembled group of vets from the doorway of the conference room. Dr. Bader nodded to him. "It looks like you've brought someone with you. Come on in and find a seat in the circle."

Cupping Paula's elbow, he ushered her over to some empty chairs next to Stan, who'd told him about the Tang. Every guy followed her progress with varying reactions that ranged from blatant male interest to disinterest, to vague hostility over a woman's presence. There were eight in the room, including Dr. Bader.

"As all of you know, you're welcome to bring anyone you like to these sessions. Walker Cody is the most recent addition to our group. Please introduce your guest."

"This is Paula Olsen. Her husband was killed in an explosion in Afghanistan eighteen months ago. She has a two-year-old son and is still dealing with issues that haven't been resolved. I told her she could address them here."

"Welcome, Mrs. Olsen. What we do here is totally informal. Anyone who has something to say can start."

As several minutes passed without anyone taking the initiative, Walker felt as if he was at a poker game. Everyone was at a different intensity level and wore a different face, but nobody was prepared to show his hand.

To his surprise, Paula went first. "It's pretty obvious my being here has stifled you gentlemen. It doesn't intimidate me, but it does make me realize men have difficulty opening up in front of a woman. Even though I was Brent's wife, he wouldn't share his war experiences with me while he was deployed. I got angry about that."

"Why?" One of the men spoke up in a surly tone. "You really wanted to know what he was doing out there in that hellhole day and night? You wanted him to tell you he'd just picked his buddy's brains off his jacket because he hadn't seen the ambush coming and it was his fault?"

"Yes," she said without flinching. "I would have preferred that to the not knowing."

He shook his head. "Your naïveté is pathetic."

Walker's hand automatically tightened into a fist.

"He went to war to protect me and Clay."

"Was he in the Reserves?"

"Yes."

"Then he never thought he'd serve time. No doubt he wanted a way to pay for his schooling and ended up being Uncle Sam's pawn before he was sent home in a body bag."

Her chin went up. "Whatever the reason that sends a man to war, the least I could do was listen to him if he wanted to tell me he was afraid so I could tell him I was afraid, too, and we'd get through it together. It hurt me to be deprived of that aspect of his life. In my anger, our communication suffered. I've been filled with guilt ever since. Can you understand that?"

"Hell no—"

"Speak for yourself!" another man interjected. "I'd have given anything if my wife had wanted to listen, but she didn't. When I got home, she wanted life to get back to the way it was before I left. It was like the three years I was gone had meant nothing to her. We split up and she took the kids."

"Sounds like your marriage wasn't in that great a shape before you left." This from a man sitting on the other side of Walker. "Mine wasn't, either. We're still separated. I don't know what's going to happen."

"I've been back five months," said the guy on Dr. Bader's right. "My wife and I are doing a little better, but she still can't sleep with me because I need noise."

"Get some headphones and listen to your iPod." Someone else threw out the suggestion.

"I tried that, but she feels shut out when I do that, so I stay in the living room on the couch and fall asleep watching TV. Then she just walks around with this hurt look in her eyes until I can't take it."

"Do you still get flashbacks?" Paula asked him.

"Yes."

"Do you think you might be using noise as an excuse to stay away from your wife in case you get one and you're afraid you might hurt her by accident?"

The room went quiet as a tomb as every guy in there stared at her.

"Now there's a thought worth investigating, Jack." Dr. Bader remarked. "Have you talked to her about them?"

"When I first got home I told her I had nightmares."

"But a flashback is different from a nightmare because they can happen anytime," Paula interjected. "Walker had one the day we met at a dog parade. After he prevented my son from getting bitten, he thought he was back in Iraq trying to save a child from a bomb about to go off.

"He ran from me because he was afraid of accidentally hurting someone in the process. Until he explained, I didn't understand, but I was never afraid of him. Your wife won't be afraid, either.

"Walker telling me what was driving him at that moment allowed me to share a little of the war with him. You can't imagine the difference that has made to me. It wouldn't occur to me not to feel safe with him."

Walker didn't know that. Her admission relieved him of a fear he'd been holding in.

"Why don't you tell your wife the truth?" Paula continued. "Sleep with her tonight without your iPod. I bet she'll be so relieved to know the real reason you want noise, she'll do anything to help you. I promise her hurt look will go away if you give her half a chance. Women can be tough, too."

The other man studied her for a minute. "I'll think about it."

"A couple of black eyes or a jab to the jaw will really endear you to her," said the most belligerent member of the group.

Paula sat forward. "She'll prefer that to being treated like a piece of crystal that only sits on a shelf to be admired. After Brent went to war and he stopped sharing, I was afraid he saw me as someone weak and diminished in his eyes. It knocked the underpinning out from under me when all along I thought we'd had a solid marriage."

In the short time Walker had known her, he'd thought he'd understood, but it took tonight's discussion to recognize the difference between intellectual and emotional understanding of her pain.

She turned her head to the man who needed help. "Naturally she couldn't share combat with you, but if you'll allow her to get inside your psyche, she'll feel more a part of your experience. My husband robbed me of that. I'm afraid I lost a lot of confidence and then took it out on him without meaning to." Her voice trembled.

Dr. Bader nodded. "Mrs. Olsen has given you guys a lot to think about."

"What if I have flashbacks for the rest of my life?" The man sounded anguished.

"What if you do?" she fired back. "Some people live with lifelong illnesses, but they and those they love deal with them."

"You know what I think?" the angry one cried out. "You're another shrink planted in here talking bullshit!"

Walker shot to his feet. "In case you've forgotten, this isn't the battlefield. You need to watch your mouth, soldier!" He checked his watch. There were fifteen minutes remaining, but he refused to subject Paula to any more. "Let's go," he muttered and clasped her hand.

She got up, ready to follow him out the door. Dr. Bader sent him a speaking glance as if to say they'd talk tomorrow at his next appointment.

When they were back in the truck, he turned to her before starting the motor. "Paula—"

"I know what you're going to say," she interrupted him. In the semidarkness of the cab her face looked flushed. "Don't *you* start treating me like a piece of crystal or I couldn't take it."

"Actually my intention was the exact opposite." He leaned across and pulled her into his arms. For a long time he simply rocked her, wanting to give comfort. "You were magnificent in there," he whispered into her silky blond hair. "The guys didn't know what hit them."

"That guy was so angry. The poor thing."

"You hit a nerve. Dr. Bader will no doubt explore it with him in private. You were good for the group." *You're good for me, Mrs. Olsen. I wish to hell you weren't.* With reluctance he let her go and turned on the ignition. "I'm hungry. What about you?"

"I'd enjoy a hamburger."

"Good." They pulled out of the parking lot and headed

for the nearest drive-through. A few minutes later they had their food and were on their way back to Cody. He looked over at her. "What are you thinking?"

She'd been munching on a French fry. "That every man who has seen military action has hang-ups. On a surface level I think I already knew it, but tonight opened my eyes a little more to the fact that Brent wasn't a unique case. That helps me. And I learned something else."

Pleased to hear that much of an admission, he said, "What was that?"

"From the beginning you were willing to admit your PTSD terrified you. I find it even more humbling that you could admit it to me. That makes you very special."

"I hardly had a choice after you caught me in the act," he said before pulling up in front of her apartment.

"You mean in the act of doing something selfless?" She smiled gently. "Thank you for letting me come to the session tonight. It's given me a lot to think about." She didn't know the half of it. "I'd like to thank you again for the lovely day at your cabin."

"Come up any time you want to paint, whether I'm there or not. This weekend if you'd like. The columbines should be out. Whites, blues, purples…"

"Oh I'd like—" she blurted, then paused. Looking disappointed, she said, "Maybe one day I'll take you up on your generous offer, but it's my father-in-law's birthday Saturday. I promised to drive to Garland on Friday and stay until Sunday night. They wish I lived there so they could see more of Clay. Naturally he's the joy of their lives."

Of course she wanted to be around Brent's parents. It kept his memory alive. Walker's hand tightened on the steering wheel. To enjoy Paula's company meant dealing with a crowd of three. What was he doing? *You're a fool, Cody.*

"Will you be going to Hugo for the rodeo?" Her question seemed to come out of the blue.

"No. My hazer and I will be competing at the Last Stand Rodeo in Coulee City, Washington."

"Sounds like you've got your work cut out for you, then." She averted her eyes and opened the door. "No—please stay where you are. I'll see myself to the door."

PAULA LET HERSELF INSIDE the apartment. "Angie!" she exclaimed. "Where's Katy?" Her friend was sitting on the couch going through a packet of correspondence.

Angie put it down. "I got accepted back into the nursing program and want your advice to make some decisions fast, so I told Katy she could go home. Don't worry. I paid her. Danice is in the guest bedroom asleep in the playpen."

"I'm so glad you're here." She sank down in one of the chairs facing the couch.

"What's wrong?"

She bit her lip. "Everything."

"Maybe you shouldn't have gone to that support group. I was afraid it might upset you too much."

Paula shook her head. "That part was fine. Enlightening even. If we had time, I'd tell you what went on, but I know you need to talk."

"We've got all night. Tell me what happened."

After Paula finished relating the details, Angie said, "I'm impressed with Walker. He's the opposite of Brent."

"In what way?"

"Instead of trying to shield you, he took you with him and threw you in the deep end of the pool, watching to see if you could swim. I guess he doesn't know yet that you were a champion swimmer for the University of Idaho." Angie sat forward. "So what's really going on with you and Walker Cody?"

"Nothing."

Her brows lifted. "I thought you just spent the past four hours with him."

"We don't have a normal relationship. I don't even know what you'd call it."

"Then what's the problem, aside from the fact that you feel you're betraying Brent's memory for being attracted to him?"

She stirred restlessly. "I wish I felt this attraction for anyone else... Matt Spurling—"

"Oh, Paula, you should hear yourself. Whatever isn't going on between you and Walker, it's not for the lack of chemistry."

"I realize that." Her head lifted. "He's gone back to competing in the rodeo."

"That's what Codys do."

"It's dangerous. His best friend died in the box."

"So if you were ever to really care for him, you could lose him like you did Brent." Angie could see right through her. "Do you know how crazy that sounds? Your mind has gone from A to Z and the two of you haven't even dated!"

Paula bowed her head. "I told you I'm a mess."

"That's because you're stuck in a groove going nowhere. If you'd allow yourself to get to know him, you'd discover he has flaws like every guy. Maybe you'd be turned off by them and all this premature angst over death wouldn't be the major issue."

Her friend was right. "You always make good sense, Angie. How am I going to handle it when you're not downstairs anymore?" She stood up. "I'll get us a couple of diet sodas from the fridge, then I want to hear about your plans."

"Before we change the subject, one piece of advice from soon-to-be Nurse Gregson here."

"What?"

"Remove your widow's shroud and give yourself permission to take up your life again, even if Brent can't. He wouldn't want you to remain in limbo, Paula. You *know* he wouldn't."

"LADIES AND GENTLEMEN—you just saw Walker Cody from Markton, Wyoming, who won his world title in 2004. Tonight he stopped the clock at 3.9 seconds, fastest time here at the Coulee Last Stand. With this kind of momentum, he's set for the Canyonlands Rodeo in Utah next weekend. Tonight Bobby Rich, number three in the world standings from Reno, Nevada, was just one-tenth of a second behind him at 4.0. This is steer wrestling at its best."

Walker could hear the announcer as he walked Peaches to the trailer parked behind the arena. Boyd walked alongside him leading his horse Jester. He kept glancing at Walker. "It was the best night for you yet. What's wrong?"

"3.9s aren't fast enough or anything close, Boyd. The Cody Roundup is only five weeks away. I'll have to put up a time of 3.4 or a 3.5 if I hope to win, and it's not going to happen."

"That's no way to talk. You beat everyone out there tonight."

"The steer cooperated and you're still the best hazer around. *I'm* the problem, Boyd. Let's face it. I'm an old man and have set myself an almost-impossible task by starting to compete so late in the season. No matter how much practice we've been putting in for the past three weeks, I can't seem to shave off any more time. That 4.0 I got in Redding was a disaster!"

"Look, Walker, you can tell me I'm out of line if you want to, but there's something else eating at you and it's putting you at a psychological disadvantage."

"I don't want to talk about it."

"That's what I mean. You've let something build in your

head without dealing with it. That's why you feel like you're off your game."

Paula was in his head. That's what was wrong. Damn if she hadn't messed with his mind since the first time he'd looked into those soulful blue eyes of hers. After the other night he decided he was through with her, but he hadn't counted on this emptiness.

"Why don't you come with me? I'm meeting some of the guys over at Phil Kennard's trailer and we're going into town."

"Thanks for the invite, but I'd be lousy company." Walker didn't want to be with a bunch of younger guys on a Saturday night. He wanted to be with Paula, but not if she couldn't get over Brent.

"Then why don't you charter a plane and fly to the ranch tonight? I'll drive the horses back tomorrow."

"You shouldn't have to do it alone."

"I'll find someone to go with me."

"You're a good man." He breathed in deeply. "If I can arrange it, I think I will get out of here tonight."

"There's nothing like your own bed if you need a good night's sleep. Do you ever get one? You know—since you've been back from Iraq?"

"Sometimes," he answered honestly.

Though Walker's bedroom in the trailer was separate from the living room hide-a-bed where Boyd slept, they were close enough that he had to be aware when Walker had one of his more restless nights.

He'd told Boyd to be prepared in case he had a flashback, but to his surprise and relief, there hadn't been any while they'd been gone. In fact there'd been no incidents for quite a while. Staying physically fit really seemed to help.

Walker felt his friend's compassion. "What can I do to help?"

"Hang in there with me. If we can hold our own next weekend, there'll be another ten thousand dollars for you."

"Why do you keep trying to throw your share of the money at me?"

"Because I don't know anyone else who'd be able to put up with me." He patted Boyd's shoulder. "I'll see you at the ranch on Monday."

PAULA AWAKENED EARLY Sunday morning realizing she couldn't stay at her in-laws any longer. She'd had a wonderful time with them. Clay had loved being with his grandparents, but the desire to visit Walker's cabin and finish her painting was so strong, she found herself packing and ready to leave by nine.

Brent's folks were understanding about her need to get back home because of work. It wasn't a lie, exactly. She always had a landscaping project waiting for her. But work wasn't what was driving her as she loaded up her Toyota and left the sleepy little hamlet for the drive back to Cody.

A series of puffy white clouds had lined up in perfect rows across the blue sky. The smell of freshly cut summer grass made her inhale deeply. She heard the sound of a tractor in the distance and the chirping of birdsong filled the car. It would be hot later, but right now the temperature and soft breeze were so delightful, she didn't need the AC.

The route took her through Powell with its recent attendant memories of going there with Walker. Within the hour her heart picked up speed as she passed beneath the arch to the Cottonwood Ranch. She took the outer perimeter road that wound up the base of Carter Mountain. Soon she reached the dirt road and began the climb, leaving the storybooklike clusters of immaculate ranch outbuildings behind.

When she'd scaled the final rise and spied his black truck parked outside the cabin, her heart thudded so fast, she could hardly breathe. He was supposed to be in Coulee, wasn't he? Maybe he'd driven there with someone else and had left his truck here.

"Do you remember this place?" she asked Clay, stopping in front of the spruce tree because one of the squirrels was scurrying around the branches, another precious memory associated with Walker. Her son smiled when he saw it and pointed his hand in its direction.

"Yes, that's right," she whispered. "We were here before." She stood still until the squirrel disappeared in the upper branches, then with Clay in her arms, she crossed the distance to the cabin. In case Walker was inside, she knocked on the door then waited a full minute. Maybe he needed time to answer it. If he was asleep, then she didn't want to knock again and wake him up.

She tried the handle. To her surprise the door gave. She poked her head inside. Silence greeted her ears.

Her glance darted to the picnic table. The case of pastels she'd given him had been left open. A few of them lay next to his drawing pad. Over on the counter she saw a jar of Tang with a mug next to it and an opened package of peanuts, the kind you bought at a convenience store. His breakfast, or a snack?

She didn't dare go inside in case she wakened him and triggered a flashback because he thought someone was trespassing. Maybe he'd gone for a morning hike and would be back soon, so that was why he'd left the door unlocked.

The best thing to do was get Clay settled in his swing so she could work on her painting. Maybe she'd see Walker before she left for the apartment.

While she was getting things out of her car, she heard footfalls behind her and turned around. Against the sun's rays she saw the silhouette of a tall flesh-and-blood man coming toward her carrying a fly rod in one hand and a fish chain with three ten-inch-size trout in the other.

"Walker…"

"Good morning." His deep voice sounded gravelly.

"I decided to take you up on your offer."

"So I see." His eyes glowed an intense green. She knew then that she hadn't done the wrong thing. "If I'd known I was going to have company this morning, I would have caught more." Clay ran toward him and grabbed his leg in a bear hug.

Walker chuckled. "I'd like to hug you, too, sport, but I've been cleaning fish. Come with me." He more or less dragged Clay along. Her little boy thought it was a game and clung harder, giggling all the way inside the cabin.

He rested his pole against the cabin, then went inside with the fish. While he washed his hands, he looked over at her. "Did you have a nice visit with your in-laws?"

"We had a good time, didn't we, Clay? His grandparents spoiled him silly, but then that was the whole point. Did you decide not to go to Washington this weekend?"

"No. I was there for two nights of competition and flew back late last night. Would you like breakfast before the *artiste* gets started outside?"

She couldn't repress a smile. "I would never turn down a fresh catch of trout."

His restless gaze wandered over her. She thought maybe he was glad to see her. "I presume everything but the kitchen sink is in your car."

Paula burst into laughter and nodded.

"I'll bring it in." He gathered Clay in his arms. "Come on, little guy. We've got work to do."

As they disappeared out the door, Paula opened the tablet on the table, curious to see what he'd added. The newest page contained an asymmetrical, dark gray blot with a purple dot at the center that took up most of the eight-by-ten paper. The next one was the same gray blot with a larger, dark purple smudge in the center.

Three more pages revealed the same gray blot, but the purple smudge was getting bigger. She wasn't surprised to see the next page revealed a perfect circle in purple. Another page was scribbled crimson red with an outline of purple. She flipped to the next drawing. Here he'd used what looked like his thumb to smear colors cascading down the page like a waterfall.

On the far left he'd chosen sunny yellow, next to it a pale blue, then a chalky white followed by a bright blue, an azure blue and a dark purple. But across it he'd punctuated the whole thing with a horizontal slash of black. He'd done it with such flourish and violence, it could be his signature.

She quickly shut it and moved the tablet and pastels to the other end of the table. For someone who didn't know how to get started, he'd expressed a lot of emotion there.

By the time Walker returned with Clay, she was setting the table. Having done all this before, they worked in perfect harmony. Before long both of them were replete with the pan-fried rainbows he'd skillfully filleted.

"That was fabulous, Walker. Clay ate his share, too. It was his first taste of trout."

"Fish puts hair on your chest," he teased him. After ruffling his blond curls, he pulled her sleepy boy out of his swing. In the process Clay's cowboy boot caught the hem of Walker's loose-fitting beige T-shirt, lifting it. For a moment Paula glimpsed the widespread scar tissue on part of his chest and running along his side to his hip beneath his jeans.

Walker intercepted her glance before putting Clay down so he could run around. She felt his defenses go up, but they couldn't hide the vulnerability in his eyes. Who would have guessed what this strong, spectacular man kept locked up from the world?

Without saying anything, she walked Clay into the bedroom. After changing his diaper, she put him down for a short nap in the playpen. When he curled up with his blanket, she drew the baby oil out of the bag and joined Walker, who was finishing the dishes.

"What have you got there?"

"Come in the living room when you're through and find out," she urged him.

That brought him out of the kitchen in a hurry. "What's going on?"

"I would like to do something nice for you, but it requires you to lie down on the couch on your side with your head at this end." Unmistakable shock broke out on his face. "Come on. Don't be shy. I won't do anything you don't want me to do."

The vulnerability in his eyes was suddenly replaced by an expectant light. "I thought I'd experienced everything there was to be experienced, but I must admit this is a first." His voice penetrated to her insides.

She smiled an almost-invisible smile. "Take off your boots and shirt. You'll be more comfortable."

"Yes, ma'am." He pulled them off in no time and stretched out so his scarred side was accessible to her. It pleased her that the jade was still fastened around his neck. Walker's hard-muscled body with its smattering of black chest hair had a male beauty she'd rarely seen in any other man. He had to know what she was thinking because his eyes never left her face.

"The doctors who put you back together with these skin grafts did amazing work. I have a younger cousin who was burned in a grass fire and had grafts done on his back. For several years after that my aunt rubbed oil into them. My mom and I took turns helping her when we could. He said it made a big difference in his comfort. Would you trust me to do that for you?"

"What do you think?"

Her brows lifted. "Just checking." She reached for the baby oil, then knelt down and began to smooth it into his skin the way she'd been taught to do. Paula lost track of time as she gently massaged every part of the scarring that was exposed.

"I smell as sweet as Clay," he muttered.

"You do." She laughed gently. "How does it feel? Am I hurting you?"

"If this is pain, then never let it stop. I think I died and woke up in paradise."

Her throat swelled. "You deserve to experience relief after what you've sacrificed." She rubbed her hands over his strong arm and shoulder, then inched along to his back and neck. With each movement she could feel the tension go out of him. No matter how small, this was one thing she could do for him, wanted to do for him.

"When do *you* get relief?" he asked sometime later when she'd thought he'd drifted off.

"Every time Clay snuggles against me."

"There's nothing like a warm, loving body, is there?"

"No," she whispered. It shocked her to realize she was aching for him to pull her into his strong arms and kiss her.

"Were you very much in love with your husband?"

The question shattered the moment for her. "Yes."

But with her hands still on Walker's body, it came to her how far she'd come from eighteen months ago when she couldn't have imagined a scene like this with another man. It hadn't been in the realm of possibility.

Paula got to her feet. She needed to wash the oil off her

hands. Walker dressed and followed her into the kitchen, his expression inscrutable. When it came to women, it appeared he tended to play his cards very close to the chest. Maybe he'd left someone special behind who still had a hold on him. Paula sighed. Forget doing any painting today.

She turned to him. "I didn't mean to stay this long and need to get home."

"I'll get Clay and help you pack up."

Within a few minutes he'd put Clay in his car seat and given him a kiss on his forehead. "See you, little guy." His unreadable gaze swiveled to hers. "Drive safely."

"I will." She glanced up at him from the driver's seat. He stood a short distance from her with his powerful legs slightly apart, looking long, dark and more dangerous than ever. "Where's your next rodeo?"

"Moab, Utah."

"Please take care of yourself," she implored, hating the throb in her voice.

"I always do. Don't forget that you can always come up here and paint. I'll leave a key at the base of the fattest blue spruce. If I'm not here, feel free to use the cabin."

He baffled her.

"Thank you, Walker," she whispered, touched by his generosity. At the same time she struggled with unassuaged needs he'd aroused. This would definitely be her last visit to the cabin.

Chapter Eight

June 2

Dr. Bader sat back in his swivel chair eyeing Walker speculatively. "I was sorry you didn't bring Paula to the group session with you last night. Her remarks did more good for Mac than three months of therapy. Thanks to her, he finally opened up to his wife about his flashbacks. They're working on their problem. Paula's welcome any time. Didn't she want to come again?"

Walker avoided his gaze. "I don't know."

"Do you think she benefited from it?"

"She said a few questions got answered." Since Paula had dropped by the cabin on Sunday, he'd been so conflicted he hardly knew which foot to put in front of the other.

"Something's wrong. Want to talk about it?"

His head reared. "I feel like her husband is always with us. She's still in love with him."

"You mean with his memory, but he has passed on. You're alive to make new memories with her. This will take time, of course."

"The last time I was with her, I—" He shook his head. "It doesn't matter."

"What happened?"

When Walker told him, he said, "You honestly think she

was confusing you with her husband when she gave you a massage?"

"No," he ground out. "I just don't need her doing me any favors because of my 'sacrifice.'"

"Then what do you want from her?"

His temper flared. "A hell of a lot more than she's capable of giving."

"She's never responded to your physical overtures?"

"I haven't made any." Giving her comfort after the other therapy session didn't count.

"So you're angry she hasn't made the right kind of overture to you." Walker squirmed. "I'd say the fact that she made one at all is rather amazing. Has it occurred to you she's afraid you're just using her as a crutch—you know, the first available woman kind of thing—until you get back to normal and move on with someone you really want?"

He lurched forward. "She couldn't think that."

"Weren't you listening to anything she said the other night? Let me refresh your memory." He turned on the tape player. Suddenly Walker was hearing Paula's voice.

If you'll allow her to get inside your psyche, she'll feel more a part of your experience. My husband robbed me of that. I'm afraid I lost a lot of confidence.

The doctor switched off the machine. "Perhaps if Paula knew more of what was going on in *your* psyche, you'd get the sign you're looking for, but that would mean taking a risk."

Dr. Bader knew him too well.

"Let's move on." He reached for Walker's drawing pad and studied the latest pictures. "Which family member is the purple one?"

Walker took a steadying breath. "My father."

"He's in every picture. What was your problem with him before you joined the military?"

Good grief. Dr. Bader was so good it was shocking. "I resented him for telling me how to live my life when his isn't perfect."

"Not perfect, as in..."

"He cheated on my mother."

"Only one man on this earth was perfect unless I've miscounted and you're the second one." Walker stirred in the chair. "Your mother forgave him?"

"I guess. They're still together."

"How long ago did it happen?"

"Early in the marriage. My mother confirmed it a few weeks ago."

"Do the others in your family know about the affair?"

"I don't think so."

"Does your father know that you know?"

"Maybe mother told him."

"Has he been good to her?"

"Yes."

"And to you?"

He eyed the other man solemnly. "Yes."

"You know what I think, Walker? Your war experiences don't come close to the pain you've suffered because of a mistake he made."

Walker groaned inwardly at the man's perception.

"By joining the military you stayed away from a sport that once upon a time brought you a great deal of enjoyment and fame. Because of what your father did, you denied yourself the camaraderie of your parents and siblings for a long time. I'm going to tell you something else about yourself. Until you can let go of your anger at him for something that happened so long ago, you'll always be conflicted."

He shut the drawing pad and pushed it toward him. "While the summer rodeo season is on, I don't expect I'll see you before next Wednesday. Keep up your physical regimen. Try to make a group session when you can. In comparison to a month ago, you're looking splendid."

PAULA HADN'T BEEN TO Zapata's for quite a while. Matt had asked her to meet him at the Mexican restaurant on Wednesday evening. He wanted to thank her on behalf of the board for the wonderful work she'd done on the landscaping project for their company and wouldn't take no for an answer. Against her better judgment, she'd agreed.

After asking Katy to babysit Clay, she arranged to meet him at six, making it clear she could only give him an hour of her time. As she feared, near the end of their meal he got around to asking her to go golfing with him at the Olive Glenn Country Club on Saturday. She'd been expecting him to ask her out socially and was ready for him.

"That sounds lovely, Matt, and I'm very flattered, but I can't go out with you because I've become involved with someone else."

His face fell. "It's serious, then?"

"Yes." Paula had no guarantees she'd ever see Walker again, but yes, it was serious for her until he was out of her blood. "I'm sorry. I hope you'll excuse me now. I need to get home to Clay."

He nodded. "Whoever he is, he's a lucky man. I'll walk you out." He left some bills on the table. "Shall we go?"

Paula knew she'd hurt his pride, but it was better Matt knew the truth tonight.

After they stood up, he ushered her to the entrance. Another group of people were headed there at the same time. That's when she saw a dark head, taller than the rest. A pair of green eyes blazing between black lashes collided with hers, stopping her in her tracks. He couldn't have missed noticing that Matt had cupped her elbow to ease her on through.

"Walker Cody," Matt said with surprise in his voice.

"Champion steer wrestler extraordinaire! I didn't know you were back from overseas."

"I've been home for a while. How are you, Matt?" The two men shook hands. Paula was stunned they knew each other.

"Terrific. Let me introduce you to this beautiful lady, Paula Olsen."

No, no, Matt… Why did he say that?

"We've met." Walker's voice came out in a lower register. "How are you, Paula?"

"I'm fine, thank you," she answered, dry-mouthed. "And you?" Like a potato too hot to handle, she tossed the conversation in his direction.

"Couldn't be better." He said it with a defiance new for him. "Where's Clay tonight?"

"With the babysitter."

His eyes had narrowed to slits. "I'm here with Ruth and Leslie Pearsoll. He's the owner of the feed and grain store in Markton."

Troy's parents… Her hand slid to her throat.

Walker turned to the older couple standing next to him. "Paula is a landscape architect with EarthDesigns here in Cody. She was the one who designed the grounds of the folks' new ranch house," he explained.

"You're kidding." Matt looked at Paula, clearly astonished. Walker was dropping his little bombs all over the place.

"And Matt Spurling here is the CEO of the Spurling Natural Gas Company. We lease our land to them."

They did? Paula's mind was reeling.

"How do you do," the Pearsolls both said, and everyone shook hands.

"Your family must be thrilled you're back." Matt's respect and admiration for Walker was palpable. "Are you going to be doing some bulldogging again?"

"As a matter of fact I've ridden in several rodeos already," Walker admitted.

With those war injuries, she couldn't imagine anything worse than putting himself in more jeopardy throwing down a bull, but as Angie said, "It's what Codys do."

"I was just talking to him about that," Mr. Pearsoll interjected. "It'll be like old times to see him in the arena again. He and our son lived for it."

Ruth nodded to Matt. "Troy and Walker were best friends before Troy was killed during the rodeo six years ago."

"Now that Walker's back, he's setting every bulldogger in the country on his ear." Mr. Pearsoll's eyes had grown moist.

Paula's emotions were in such deep turmoil, she needed to get out of there. "It was very nice to meet you," she said to the Pearsolls. "Nice to see you too, Walker." Not daring to look at him, she left the restaurant with Matt.

He followed her across the street to her car. "All the Codys are winners, but as my dad once told me, Walker had an edge that made him a formidable opponent. Did you ever see him in action?"

"No."

"He could bring down a steer so fast, it was hair-raising. People were really surprised when he went into the Marines."

Paula was relieved to get behind the wheel. If she had to listen to Matt say one more thing about Walker, she was going to go to pieces. "The dinner was lovely, Matt. Thank you for giving me the opportunity to do the landscaping project for your company."

"You know how we feel. *I* feel," he added, eyeing her soberly. "Good luck to you, Paula."

"You, too."

As he walked off, she backed out and drove home as fast

as she could without getting a speeding ticket. Katy must have heard her come in the door because she rushed into the living room.

"I'm glad you're home! Clay started coughing a few minutes ago. When I went in to him, he'd thrown up. I was just going to take his temperature because he feels hot."

"That came on fast. He seemed fine before I left. Thanks for being such a good sitter." She opened her purse and paid her.

"I hope he'll be all right. See you."

Paula saw her to the door, then hurried into the nursery. Sure enough Clay had a temperature of 101. While she was holding him, he threw up again and wouldn't stop crying. This was so unusual for him she couldn't sit around and wonder what was wrong. The only thing to do was take him over to nighttime pediatrics.

She grabbed his baby bag and a clean blanket. Once she'd found her purse, she left the apartment, only to meet Walker who was coming up the steps two at a time with purpose. But one look at her crying child and a grimace broke out on his features. "What's wrong with Clay?"

"I don't know. I walked in the house to find him running a temperature and throwing up. I've never seen him get sick this fast. He needs a doctor."

"I'll drive you in your car so you can sit in back with him. Give me your purse."

"Thank you, Walker." She handed it to him so he could get the keys. Whatever reason had brought him over, she was thankful he'd come. "The Madsen Clinic stays open all night."

"I know." He strapped Clay in his car seat, then helped her in back. Inside of five minutes he'd driven them to the clinic and had accompanied her inside. Clay was sick again on the way in. "He hates throwing up. It scares him."

"Poor little guy. Let me hold him while you sign in."

To have him here was such a relief, she didn't know what she would have done without him. After she'd talked to the receptionist, she hurried over to where he was walking with Clay in the crowded waiting room.

The sight of him cuddling her sick son, who'd burrowed against him while Walker rubbed his little back and talked to him, filled her heart with warmth.

Five more minutes and a nurse came through the doors calling for Olsen.

"I'm going in with you," Walker announced.

"I want you to." At this stage there'd be no prying Clay away from him.

They were shown to one of the rooms. When the harried-looking doctor came in, her son clung to Walker, who sat down on the chair with him so an examination could take place.

After a few minutes he said, "He's got a double ear infection."

"Is it serious?" Walker sounded anxious.

"I've seen a lot of these tonight, Mr. Olsen." To hear the doctor address Walker that way took Paula's breath. "A bug is going around. We'll get him started on an antibiotic. When you get home, push fluids. Give him some Pedialyte and Children's Tylenol. He should be all right. If his temperature should go higher, bring him back."

The clinic was so busy, the doctor didn't have a lot of time to talk. As soon as he wrote out the prescriptions, Walker took them and they left the clinic. "I'll drive you home, then run to the pharmacy and fill these."

"You don't have to do that."

His lips thinned. "Would you rather I didn't?"

"I didn't say that. It's just that—"

"I'm not *Mr.* Olsen?" He cut her off in a frigid tone before settling her and Clay in the car once more.

When he was behind the wheel she said, "Please don't put words in my mouth. You have no idea how grateful I am you're with me. I just don't want you to think I'm taking advantage."

She could see his piercing eyes through the rearview mirror. "I like helping. Clay and I have fought off black bears and eaten rainbow trout together. We're buddies."

"I know you are." *I know.* "When you're at the pharmacy, will you try to get cherry Pedialyte? He likes that flavor."

"Can you think of anything else you need?"

"Not right now."

They'd reached the apartment. He helped them inside, then took off with that speed she associated with him. While he was gone, she bathed Clay and put a clean shirt and diaper on him. Her little angel still whimpered against her, but hadn't thrown up again.

She walked around with him and sang songs until Walker's return. He rushed inside the kitchen and got everything out of the sacks.

"Why don't you give Clay his meds while I hold him?"

The suggestion seemed to appease Walker. With the expertise of a father who'd done this for years, he filled a clean bottle with the Pedialyte.

By tacit agreement they went in the living room and sat down on the couch. Clay drank a little, then pushed the bottle away. They took turns holding him. Finally he consumed a fairly good portion, and Paula put him in his crib with a fresh blanket. "Go to sleep, sweetheart."

When they went back out to the living room, Paula felt limp as a rag. She looked over at Walker who, despite their ordeal, looked fabulous in a silky black sport shirt and gray trousers. "All I ever do is thank you. You were wonderful with him tonight. He's perfectly content with you."

"Clay's a special boy. If you need any help, I want you to call me even if it's in the middle of the night. Is there something I can write on and I'll give you my cell phone number?"

It was hard to believe they'd known each other for a month and she still didn't have his number. "Tell me what it is and I'll program it into my cell." She pulled the phone out of her purse.

When that was done he said, "Tonight I wanted to talk to you and took a chance on your coming straight home to Clay after you left the restaurant earlier."

"I'm glad you did," she said in an emotion-filled voice.

He studied her features through veiled eyes. Something serious was on his mind. "What does Matt Spurling mean to you?"

His question caught her off guard, but it deserved an honest answer. "Matt's a recent client who would like to be more than that."

"The man made that obvious. I thought he was married."

"They were divorced some time ago."

Walker cocked his dark head. "When you drove away from the restaurant in your car, I noticed he didn't follow, but maybe you're expecting him later tonight. If I'm in the way, just say so."

Heat filled her cheeks. "Of course you're not! How could you even think it? If you remember, I drove up to your cabin last Sunday."

"I recall it very well," his voice grated, "including the be-nice-to-a-vet massage. Is that what the unexpected drop-in was all about?"

She blinked. "You think I feel sorry for you?"

"*Don't* you?" he bit out.

"That's the *last* emotion you bring out in me."

His hands shot to her upper arms. "What's the first?" he fired.

"Walker…"

"You can't tell me, can you? Maybe this will help." His dark head lowered, blotting out the light from the lamp.

With a low moan, Paula surrendered her mouth to him in an explosion of need. For so long she'd fought against this happening, but at the first taste of him she couldn't have held back if she'd wanted to. As though in an avalanche gaining momentum, she was caught in a force beyond her control.

This was no brief kiss. His mouth kindled a hunger inside her that grew even as it was being appeased. Walker couldn't seem to get enough of her, either. One kiss became another and another, none of them long enough or deep enough as this fusion of mouths and bodies sent her into a swirling rapture.

Those bronzed hands slid into her silky hair, cupping her head to give him easier access to her eyes and mouth. She clung to him, delirious with wanting. Desire shot through her like white-hot flame. He crushed her against him, then brought a protesting groan from her as he set her away from him without warning. The abrupt cessation of ecstasy produced literal pain.

His eyes had gone dark, confusing her. "Brent was a lucky man. Matt doesn't have a clue what he's up against, does he?" After another kiss to her swollen lips, he was gone.

She stood there dazed and weaving. *Brent was a lucky man?*

Paula couldn't keep up with his thought processes. First he'd accused her of feeling sorry for him; now he thought she was using him and Matt as substitutes for her husband?

A cry of anger escaped her throat before she went to the nursery to check on Clay.

AFTER A WRETCHED NIGHT, Walker woke up Thursday morning totally out of sorts. A shower and shave didn't help his state of mind. Once he'd dressed in a clean T-shirt and jeans, he burst into the kitchen still fit to be tied. Before he did anything else, he drank two cups of coffee with a ton of sugar.

Besides worrying about Clay, seeing Matt Spurling with Paula at the restaurant had been like getting impaled on a steer horn. Walker's arrogance and naïveté had led him to assume he was the only man in her life. *Mortal* man, he amended bleakly.

Of course she had male clients, but when he'd watched Matt looking at her with undeniable male interest, he lost his perspective and later came close to losing complete control while he was kissing her senseless. Hell, hell and hell.

He grabbed his cell and charged out of the cabin ready to wreck shop. On the way down the mountain he drove the truck so hard it shimmied half a dozen times. But the second he came out on paved road, he was forced to slam on his brakes because he suddenly remembered that he needed to call Boyd.

His hazer was waiting for him at the arena. They'd planned to practice with some steers this morning, but this was one time Walker wouldn't be able to make it. Depending on how Clay was doing, they might not be able to leave for Canyonlands until tonight. He needed to get to Paula's apartment pronto, not only to help with Clay, but to try and repair the damage he'd done.

Not wanting to arrive empty-handed, he turned around and went back to the cabin. After rustling up a Mason jar, he filled it with as much Indian paintbrush as it would hold and placed it on the floor of the cab.

By now he'd calmed down enough to drive to Cody without breaking a tire rod. He'd planned to pick up a present for Clay in town, but when he passed Whittaker's gift shop, he made a U-turn and pulled up in front.

Walker climbed down from the cab and walked past a couple of tourists coming out the door. Old man Whittaker was busy stacking Buffalo Bill T-shirts on a shelf.

"Good morning, Tom."

He turned. "Well I'll be. If it isn't Walker Cody back from Iraq!" They shook hands. "How are you doing, son?"

That was the ten-million-dollar question. "I'm fine. You look well, sir."

"Can't complain. What can I do for you?"

"I need a present for a two-year-old boy. Maybe a stuffed animal. He's scared of dogs and bears."

The owner looked closer at him. "Is he blond?"

"Yes." Walker couldn't imagine why he'd asked the question.

"I know the little feller you mean. Big blue eyes. Cute as all get-out."

That described Clay. Maybe Tom was losing it, too, but Walker played along with him. "How do you know that?"

"About a month ago, the boy's mother bought the jade from me that's hanging around your neck. When I asked her what she was doing out in these parts, she said she was looking for a man who might be a Cody." He grinned. "Looks like she found you."

Walker's hand went automatically to the charm. "That she did," he murmured, fingering it. But he'd made it damned difficult for her.

"I keep the stuffed animals down at the other end." Walker followed him. "I've got all kinds. Beavers, squirrels, deer, elk, bison, rabbits, ducks." The owner had an amazing collection. "See anything you like?"

"Not yet."

"I've got some boxed horses. They're more expensive." He reached under the counter. "This one says it's an Appaloosa." Tom took the top off. In the tissue lay a black leopard filly.

It was adorable, like Clay. Soft to the touch. Not in the least scary. The perfect size for him to get his hand around. "I'll take it."

"Good. Do you want me to gift wrap it?"

"I don't think so. Just put it in a sack."

They moved back to the register, and Walker handed him a couple of bills.

"There you go." Tom put a little plastic whistle in the sack and handed it to him. "Tell the boy's mother that's another little present from me. When he blows on it, she'll know where he is. No wonder he's so good-looking. She's a real beauty, that one."

Yup. One glimpse into those dazed blue eyes looking up at him a month ago and he hadn't been the same since.

"Thanks, Tom."

"Don't be a stranger."

"I won't. Take care of yourself." He had one more errand to run before he drove to her apartment.

Chapter Nine

When the doorbell rang, Paula had just set Clay down on a
quilt in the living room to play with a set of different-size
buckets. She got up and walked over to the door.

"Who is it?"

"I'll give you one guess."

Her body started to tremble with excitement. She'd know
that deep, compelling voice anywhere. His parting comments
after the heady kisses she'd experienced in his arms had
given her insomnia. By early this morning she'd come to the
conclusion that only time would convince Walker there was
no one else she was kissing last night but him.

She opened the door, then had to catch her breath because
he looked so incredible in a sage-colored Polo shirt she hadn't
seen him wear before. His tan was deepening and he'd started
to fill out. Their eyes met. Today his were a clear green, not
like last night.

"C-come in," her voice faltered.

He moved his hard-muscled body inside, bringing his own
enticing male scent with him. "How's Clay?"

"As you can see, he's doing a little better."

"Did he sleep?"

"Yes, and he hasn't thrown up since the clinic, but he's
still running a temperature, though it's not as high."

"That's a relief." He reached inside one of the sacks he

was holding and brought out a soft-looking stuffed animal. It was a little white pony with black spots and a short tail.

"Oh, how darling! Look, Clay…"

Walker hunkered down by the quilt. "Hey, sport. What do you think?" He handed the toy to her son, who gave him an angelic smile, then took it and immediately put the head in his mouth.

They both laughed. He got up and turned to her. "These are for us."

She took the other sack from him and looked inside. "Bagels and cream cheese! Just what the doctor ordered. I haven't had breakfast yet."

"Neither have I."

"Then come in the kitchen and I'll make us some eggs to go with them."

Before he'd rung the doorbell, she'd been in the depths over the situation with him. For him to show up so unexpectedly brightened her day. Somehow she had to convince him he could never be a substitute for anyone.

"I need to bring something else in from the truck. I'll be back in a minute to keep an eye on Clay."

"Thanks, but you don't have to worry about him. I've got this place baby-proofed. He can't get in too much trouble around here."

While she heated the grill and got the eggs ready to cook, Walker entered the kitchen, his arms full of Indian paintbrush.

A gasp escaped her throat. "Oh—how glorious!"

She saw a gleam of satisfaction in his eyes as he filled the jar with water. "Since you didn't get a chance to work on your painting the other day, I thought I'd bring the meadow to you."

"Walker…" Her feelings ran so deep, she needed another way to express them, but Clay came in the kitchen just then carrying his pony. He toddled right over to Walker, who picked him up and hugged him hard. Her son recognized him for exactly who he was and thrived under all that male attention...and affection. Emotions were threatening to drown her.

"If you want to put him in his high chair, I'll pour you some orange juice."

"I think I'll keep him on my lap. Before I leave, I want to hear him say *horse*."

She laughed. "Good luck. So far it's pretty much mumbo jumbo. You're a man after my father's heart. He can't wait until Clay is old enough to ride on his own horse with his grandpa."

"Do you see your family often?"

"Probably every six weeks or so." A moment later, she served the eggs and sat down.

Her son seemed perfectly content to stay where he was. Though he didn't have an appetite, there was nothing wrong with Walker's. He ate several helpings of everything while he talked to Clay with amazing patience.

"Hey, sport, maybe one day when you're older, you'll want to go riding with me."

Clay looked up at him. He might not understand all Walker's words, but the kind tone had captured his attention. Walker kissed his curls. "There's nothing like seeing the world from the back of a horse just like this. Let's name him. He's got so many spots, how about Pebbles? Maybe that'll be easier to say than horse."

The domestic scene was heartwarming, but frightening, as well, because she was starting to care too much for a man who risked death every time he entered the arena.

She'd made the mistake of looking at a video on YouTube Kip had told her about. Someone who'd been to the Cody Roundup six years ago had posted it. To her horror, it was a clip of Troy Pearsoll's fatal accident in the box on the Fourth of July. The video ended before death was pronounced.

Kip couldn't have known how it would affect her. Walker Cody was one of her brother's idols. He didn't realize that seeing the actual footage had been a traumatic experience for her. She'd only watched it once, unable to bring herself to replay it.

Walker had been there competing that night. To see his best friend's life snuffed out in an instant had to have come as a horrendous blow. The thought of Walk—

"Paula?" His voice broke in on her torturous thoughts. "What's wrong? You're so quiet."

Pull yourself together, Paula. "I didn't want to interrupt the fascinating conversation you two are having. You've won yourself an admirer, you know."

His eyes wandered over her features as if he were searching for another answer, but couldn't find it. "Last night he had me worried. Today he's a different boy."

"Children are resilient, thank heaven. He'll be all better in a few days."

While Walker's eyes were still probing hers, the answering machine sounded, and Matt Spurling's voice filled the kitchen.

"Hi, Paula. Please don't worry. I got the message last night. This is the last time you'll ever hear from me. I just wanted you to know I think you're a terrific person. I envy the guy. Of course this doesn't change anything. You're a master landscape architect. I hope you'll always consider me a friend."

Paula groaned. She should have turned off her answering machine earlier, but it never occurred to her Matt would call her again.

Walker shot her an inscrutable glance as he gently placed Clay on the floor. "I'll make this easy for you and leave so you can get back to your work." Suddenly the chair scraped and Walker was on his feet.

Oh no you don't.

By now Clay had pulled open the bottom kitchen drawer where she kept the rolling pin and wooden spoons he liked to play with. He put the pony inside and closed the drawer, then opened it again and pulled it out, a tedious process enjoyable only to a child.

"I'm sorry you had to hear that, Walker."

He stared at her as if he'd never seen her before. "I know how he feels," he whispered in a fierce tone. "Matt's a good man."

"That's why I didn't let things get started with him, because he *is* a good man. The problem is, I knew after we had our first business dinner together that he wanted to ask me out. From then on I discouraged him, but I couldn't avoid our final dinner last evening." She took a fortifying breath. "I was never interested in him and *you* know why."

If that didn't do something to clear up any questions Walker needed answers to, then nothing else would, but he didn't say anything and that frustrated her. What was going on in his head? "Since you've never volunteered, maybe I should be asking you about the women in your life."

He blinked. "You want a list? I've known my share and have had relationships with several."

"I'm talking about right now," she said quietly.

"What do you think I'm doing at your apartment?"

"Then you know from Matt's phone call he was never on my radar."

His features hardened. "But we both know the guy who *is*."

Not that again. "Yes—we do," she cried out in a rare display of anger. Surely he'd figured out by now that *he* was the guy in her new life. Brent would always belong to the old.

Clay must have picked up on the tension. He made noises for Walker to pick him up. He still had the pony clutched in his little fist. Walker reached down and pressed him against his chest. She noted inconsequently that her son went straight for the jade piece around his neck.

Silence stretched between them before Walker blurted, "I've got to go."

Oh, really! That was rich. Now that he'd worked out the riddle for himself, he was scared to death! Walker Cody had never been roped in by a woman. So far none of the Cody men had been permanently trapped in a female's clutches. Now that she'd pulled a fast one on him, it appeared he didn't like the feeling.

"That's no surprise," she blurted. "You do that on a regular basis, but I'm used to it. Thank you for caring so much about Clay." She fought to calm down. "He loves his gift. I love mine. Come again when you're in the mood. Next time plan to stay longer."

His lips went white around the edges. "It's not what you think, Paula."

"What do you think I'm thinking?"

"That I haven't told you everything about me."

"I haven't told you everything about me, either. We hardly know each other!"

"After last night, that's not exactly true," he said in a husky tone. She knew what he meant of course and couldn't deny it. "Now that I'm out of the military, I'm not the best bet for any woman."

Her brows furrowed. What was he getting at? "For the sake of argument, why?"

"For one thing, I'm probably sterile after being exposed to a chemical agent."

She moaned inwardly for his pain. That kind of news had to be as hard on a man as a woman. He'd been so great with

Clay, she'd thought more than once what a wonderful father he'd make one day.

"For your sake I'm sorry to hear that, but the right woman will love you, warts and all. Was there anything else you think I'm thinking?"

He rubbed the side of his jaw with his palm as if her comment had frustrated him. "Just so we understand each other, now that I can see Clay is doing better, I've got to get some practice in today. Tonight Boyd and I will be heading out to Moab in the trailer with the horses."

Though he had a legitimate reason for leaving, she knew it wasn't the whole truth. He still hadn't come completely clean with her. But as he'd admitted to Clay, Walker needed gentling first, so she would have to be patient until he was ready to tell her about any other hidden demons.

She had one of her own. Just the thought of the rodeo caused the pit in her stomach to get bigger. "Since I've seen your scars, I can't help but wonder if you're physically up to the weekly strain of competition this soon after being released from the hospital."

His dark head reared. "Sure I am. Each day that I ride and practice, my body gets stronger."

There was no *sure* about it, but she was talking to a Cody. If they could still breathe, the rodeo went on. That's what she'd heard J.W. say on one occasion. Elly was a case in point. Walker couldn't have had a tougher mentor than the man who'd forced him to ride a horse when he was Clay's age. Somehow he'd braved it through because Walker was an extraordinary male.

She rubbed her arms nervously. "I'm glad you're feeling so fit."

"Me, too. The doctor told me consistent exercise is the key to getting back."

"That may be true, but there's exercise, and then there's

the possibility of getting gored or dragged to a pulp." She couldn't seem to let it go. After the horror of his IED injury, she couldn't bear the thought of him ending up in the hospital again. Troy didn't even make it that far....

His black brows lifted. "Then it means I'll have to make certain that doesn't happen."

Oh, Walker. "To each his own poison, I guess."

Walker let go with a devil-may-care laugh. He seemed to be going through a new phase she didn't understand. She took Clay from his arms. "Excuse me for a minute while I put him down for his nap."

Paula moved past him and headed for the nursery. He followed. "If Clay weren't sick, I'd invite both of you to drive to Utah with us and watch the rodeo. Given a chance, you might discover you like it."

"That's what Kip always tells me."

"Your brother makes sense."

Keep things light, Paula. "I'll make a deal with you. If you start competing here in Cody, I'll come and watch one."

"Now that it's June, the rodeo is on every night. Starting next Monday I'll be competing most nights here just for the practice. A week from Saturday there'll be some big names coming in for substantial prize money."

Meaning it would be a big deal. A shiver ran down her spine. "Then I'll come on Saturday."

"Good."

Walker stood in the doorway while she gave Clay his medicine. Then she lowered him to the crib and handed him the bottle of Pedialyte he hadn't finished earlier. His hand still held the pony. "Go to sleep, sweetheart. I'll see you later."

When she reached the hallway, Walker blocked her progress and ended up trapping her against the wall with both hands on either side of her blond head. "Since I won't be seeing you until I'm back from Canyonlands, I just want..."

His mouth fell on hers and proceeded to devour her until the ache for him became overpowering. "Walker," she moaned his name. She knew she shouldn't be doing this, but she needed desperately to get closer to him. In a convulsive move, her arms slid around his neck

"You feel so good," he whispered on a ragged breath while he molded her to his hard, lean body. At the moment when her limbs seemed to dissolve, he tore his lips from hers and put her gently but firmly away from him.

Like lightning he moved to the living room, then paused and turned around. His green eyes looked faintly glazed. "I almost forgot. Tom Whittaker told me to give you this."

She watched him pull a blue-and-white plastic toy out of his jeans. He reached for her hand and pressed it into the palm. "When you bought my jade charm, you made a real hit with him. This is a whistle for Clay, but if he gets worse or you need help, I expect you to use it. The second I hear it, I'll come."

He cupped her face in his hands and gave her one more hungry kiss before disappearing out the front door.

When she'd recovered enough to move, she looked out the window, but he was already gone. Slowly she staggered to the kitchen to clean up. The sight of the brilliant paintbrush brought a bittersweet pain to her heart. She clung to the edge of the counter as a sob rose in her throat.

Paula squeezed the whistle tighter. If only it were a magic whistle she could blow and he'd turn back from certain danger.

Maybe her reaction was over-the-top, but steer wrestling was perilous. By returning to the rodeo circuit, Walker willingly embraced it. Every time his horse exploded from the box, he took his life in his hands. That's what the Cody family did, night after night, round after round.

Work! Paula had a ton to do. Housework. Landscaping

designs. Her art project. If she immersed herself, she might
make it through until the next time she saw Walker again. *If*
she saw him again.

ON HIS WAY TO THE CABIN to get packed for his trip, Walker
parked in front of the ranch office and went inside carrying
a folder he'd brought in the truck with him. The receptionist
lifted her head. "Walker? It's good to see you, you handsome
devil!"

"Hi, Doris. It's good to see you, too. You haven't changed
a bit. How do you stay so young?"

"You can tell a white lie better than anyone I know, but
it's still nice to hear. Were you looking for Jesse?"

"Not right now. Is my father in?"

"Yes, and there's no one with him. Go on back."

Walker walked down the hall and tapped on the door
before going in. Once inside, the surprise on his father's face
revealed how little communication there'd been between them
on a one-on-one basis since his teens. Though they'd been
together at the past two rodeos and the house, this was the
first time he'd stepped foot inside J.W.'s inner sanctum here
at the ranch office.

His father started to get to his feet, but Walker told him to
stay put. The less he had to put pressure on his bad leg, the
better. "If you're expecting someone, I'll come back another
time."

His father emoted a strange combination of trepidation and
pleasure. "Every day I've been hoping you'd walk in here. Sit
down, son. You make me nervous standing there like you're
walking on hot coals."

Maybe that was because their fiery exchanges always
ended with no resolution, but he refrained from saying anything this time and sat in one of the deep leather chairs opposite the desk.

"The twins told me you were leaving for Canyonlands today."

"Boyd and I will be heading out with the horses tonight."

His dad gave him a rare smile. "Do you have any idea how proud I am of you for getting back to bulldogging? Your speed is clocking faster with every competition. I must confess I didn't think the talk we had at the barbecue a few weeks ago did any good."

It was just like his father to take credit for something he had nothing to do with, but instead of reacting as he'd done in the past by walking out on him, Walker took a deep breath and tried to view his father dispassionately. He had to admit it was the hardest thing he'd ever had to do, to sit there and take it. Still, his conscience, unearthed by Dr. Bader, had reminded him that no man was perfect.

"Have you given more thought to running the Corriente bulls operation? No one has a better eye for them than you. Dex said a couple of draggers had slipped in with the last bunch. If you were in charge, that wouldn't happen."

Walker stretched and crossed his boot-clad feet at the ankles. "I appreciate your confidence in me, Dad, but that's not why I came in. There's something else I want to talk to you about. It's not along any of the lines you've been thinking."

The comment caused his father to press his fingertips together. He always did that when he was trying to hold his tongue. "Go on."

"The idea came to me while I was in college, but for obvious reasons I haven't been able to do anything about it until now." The real reason was seated in front of him, of course, but Walker needed to put the enmity of the past behind him or his life *would* be a desert.

"If you're thinking of opening up one of the old mines,

I had this conversation with you boys years ago. You know my feelings on it. Too risky, too expensive, too much trouble. We don't need that headache."

No, because when J.W. didn't like an idea, he refused to discuss it and that was it. Walker sat forward. "I've brought something with me I want you to read. It won't take too long." He handed him a copy of the senior paper he'd turned in to his college professor over six years ago.

His father eyed him shrewdly before settling back in his leather chair to peruse it.

Five minutes turned into fifteen before he lifted his head. It was a miracle in itself that he'd stayed with it that long. Walker heard him clear his throat, but no words came out.

He decided to take the proverbial bull by the horns.

"Because of the alarming findings about the existing natural-gas field, *if* you're willing, I'd like your permission to drill for natural gas on another part of the property."

The quiet was all consuming while his father took in what Walker had just proposed. Besides the rodeo, J.W. had always been so focused on the running of the ranch, the horses, the cattle… The idea of exploring for more gas came as the second astonishing surprise of the day for his parent, Walker's presence in his office being the first.

J.W. sat forward. "You honestly think there might be another field?"

Incredible. It seemed Walker had managed to grab his attention. "Why not? The wells in activity are located on the rangeland, away from the mountains because of the uplift. We've got rangeland to spare. Why wouldn't there be more?"

His father let out a laughing cry. "By damn, why not!"

Encouraged, Walker said, "Here's what I can see happening. If we strike a new field like the one found years ago, then I'd like to start up the J. W. Cody Natural Gas Company."

The gleam in his father's eyes grew brighter.

"But even if my theory proves wrong, we can still form our own company after the lease is up for renewal with Spurlings next year. That's not very far away."

"You know, you're right." While his father's mind was starting to get the picture, Walker was still reeling from Paula's assertion that she'd never been interested in Matt Spurling. The poor devil had taken his defeat gracefully. Hearing his voice on her answering machine had made a new man of Walker. If that made him some kind of monster, he didn't care.

"We'll keep it going until we've exhausted what's left of the field. I see no reason to go on giving away the natural resources on our land when we could be in business for ourselves and reap all the profits."

J.W. pounded his fist on the desktop. "I should have thought of it years ago." He sounded upset with himself. That wasn't the reaction Walker wanted to provoke. His father had done more to ensure the future of the Cody legacy than any Cody that went before him.

"You had other weighty matters on your mind, Dad. But think about this—every month, if it's a peak month—we make a royalty of fifteen percent of the take. That normally adds up to $200,000 a month, right?" His father nodded. "Think if we could keep the other eighty-five percent, too. We would be talking over a million dollars a month for each well."

"My brilliant son is teaching his father!"

Was this the same father who'd been down on him from day one?

"I'll tell you who was brilliant, Dad. It was our ancestor who got all the rights to the land in the first place so the government couldn't step in and control things. We own a lot more of the same kind of land where the first field was found. I've ridden Peaches all over it."

"I didn't know that." His father sounded shocked. "If you'd told me, I would have ridden out there with you."

"I had to work out my plans first, and I do it better alone."

J.W. made a strange sound in his throat. "You're my son all right."

"Just so you know, I've been investing my money since I went into the military. I've got enough to drill a couple of wildcat wells doing subsurface mapping and seismic measurements. The figures in my paper will have changed over the past six years. According to the research I've already done, it will cost three million dollars to drill for one well in today's economy."

"I'll match your funds."

He couldn't believe what he was hearing. "Thanks, but I'd like to see this project through on my own steam."

"Good for you."

"A road will have to be built for each one. If I find gas, the delineation well will tell me how big the field is underneath the ground. If we find a lot of gas, I'll have them made into development wells.

"You saw the graphics in my paper. They'll have to be forty-five acres apart, but the good thing is they're quiet and have very little physical impact on the environment except for a road. I believe it's worth pursuing."

"Worth pursuing? It's vital!" His father leaped out of his chair, grabbed his cane and came around to the front of the desk to hug Walker. "I always knew you were the brainy one in the family, but right now we're talking pure genius here."

For the first time ever, Walker saw his father totally excited about something else besides the rodeo.

He grabbed Walker's shoulder. "And you promise to live here and run the whole thing?"

"If it has your approval."

"If?" he exclaimed. "To live to an old age with all my children and grandchildren around is all I've ever wanted, son!"

The truth of his words caused a sudden surge of affection for his father that seemed to spring out of nowhere, surprising the hell out of him.

"You can talk to Mom about it, but until I've done more groundwork with a couple of engineers, let's keep this under our hats where the others are concerned."

"Agreed, but come on home with me now and we'll tell her together."

Whatever the state of his parents' marriage, it appeared they were still a team.

Walker got to his feet. "I would, but I've got to get ready to leave with Boyd. We'll talk to her when I get back."

He nodded. "Did you know Jesse's on for both nights in Hugo?"

"I figured as much, and where Jesse goes Mark Hansen follows." Walker was convinced Mark was out for blood, or Jesse would have laughed it off by now.

J.W. went oddly quiet. Evidently his father had concerns in that department, as well. He squinted at Walker. "You noticed that, too."

"Yup. I think he's shaken Jesse's confidence. Somehow I always thought of my brother as invulnerable."

"We're all vulnerable somewhere, sometime, but then we get back on track and don't look back."

"That's true," Walker murmured, wondering if this was the closest his father would ever come to confessing what he'd done. "We all saw Mark's performance in Redding. I hate to admit it, but he's good."

"He is," his father agreed, albeit reluctantly. "That's the reason I'm glad you're home for good. All my children need to support each other."

"I hear you. See you later, Dad."

Walker wished Paula and Clay were driving with him tonight. After she'd been to a few rodeos and knew what to look for, she'd get over her concerns about it being dangerous.

WHILE PAULA WAS ON THE phone with a client, she heard the high-pitched whines of some sport bikes coming down her street. Normally things were fairly quiet in her residential neighborhood. She got up from the dining room table to look out the window. Two guys pulled up in front of the apartment and parked.

As soon as she saw the familiar silver-and-black GSX-R1000 loaded with gear, she realized who it was and flew past Clay, who was sitting in front of his blocks chewing on them.

"Kip!" she cried out in delight after opening the front door. Of course she was thrilled to see him, but she'd been hoping Walker would come. He'd called every day checking up on Clay. He'd even talked to her son on the phone. But on his last call he told her they'd been delayed by a mechanical problem with the trailer. She might not see him before Tuesday.

"Hey, Pollywog!" Her older brother pulled off his helmet to reveal a thick head of dark blond hair. His grin was as big as all outdoors. With his light blue eyes and bronzed complexion, he was growing to look more like their attractive father every day. They met halfway on the stairs in a big hug.

She'd never thought about his height before, but after Walker had trapped her in the hall on Thursday, she realized the men in her family, including Brent, were shorter. Not that it mattered, but she couldn't help making the comparison.

"Why didn't you tell me you guys were coming? I'd have had dinner ready for you. Come on in."

They followed her up the rest of the stairs and entered the apartment. "How are you, Ross?" She gave his sandy-haired friend a hug. He and Kip had been best friends for years.

"Never better."

Kip dived straight for Clay and scooped him up off the floor. "Hey, little buddy. Have you missed your Uncle Kip?"

"Of course he has!"

While he held Clay he said, "We were going to do some hiking in Yellowstone Park and camp out tonight, but then it started to rain and probably won't let up until tomorrow. Since we don't have to get back home until Wednesday, we thought we'd drive here and bug you before we move on."

"I've never been happier to see anybody." The guys would help keep her mind off Walker, who'd survived another rodeo in one piece. "You can stay here tonight. I'll whip up your favorite steak fajitas." Katy had watched her boy long enough for Paula to get to the grocery store. "Clay will love it that you're here. He's getting over double earaches and is bored with my company."

"Yeah?" He poked Clay's tummy playfully. "Have you been sick?"

"While you guys freshen up in the bathroom, I'll get dinner started."

"Thanks, Paula." Ross disappeared down the hall. Kip followed her into the kitchen with Clay.

The little pony was lying on the floor with some cars next to the drawer where Clay had been playing. Kip reached for it. "This is cute." Clay immediately took it from him and jammed the head in his mouth. When Kip pulled on it, Clay kept it locked tight in his fist.

"His name is Pebbles."

Her brother chuckled. "Will you look at that? He knows what he wants."

"Walker brought it by for him the other day. Since then he hasn't let it out of his sight."

Her brother's eyes danced. "So…"

"So nothing. We're friends." No more getting physical with Walker. She couldn't afford to take the risk of caring about him any more than she already did.

"I wish *I* had a friend who lit up at the sound of my name the way you just did."

"I did not." Avoiding his merciless scrutiny, she got the steak and vegetables out of the fridge to slice. When she heard the doorbell ring, Ross called out, "I'll answer it!"

It was probably Angie. Too late to intercept him, she hurried into the living room in time to see a smooth-shaven Walker at the door wearing a coffee-brown Western shirt and jeans. He was such a striking male that, as usual, she could hardly breathe. If this was going to be her reaction every time she saw him, she'd better stock up on oxygen to help her survive.

That dark, brooding expression broke out on his face. "I've come at a bad time."

Since he'd never met Kip, she knew Walker would leap to another erroneous conclusion, but this time she was ready for him. "It's the perfect time! Please come in and meet my brother, Kip Lund, and his best friend, Ross Fenton. They rode over here on their sport bikes after getting rained out in Yellowstone Park. Tonight they're going to sleep on my living-room floor in their bedrolls."

No longer in prebattle mode as she'd come to describe him when his body tautened, Walker moved inside and shut the door. Kip gravitated to him. "It's an honor to meet you, Mr. Cody." He shook his hand, still holding Clay. "Before you left the rodeo circuit, I followed your career for years."

"So did I," Ross echoed and extended his hand. They both looked as if they'd won the lottery.

Suddenly Clay wanted out of Kip's arms and launched himself at Walker with the enthusiasm of a child greeting his father. Walker, who displayed that same physical mastery he'd shown at the dog parade, caught Clay against his chest in a loving hug before he could fall.

While Clay found the jade charm and tried to eat it, her brother sent Paula a private look that spoke volumes. She felt her face flush. "You're a hero to these guys, Walker, so don't go all modest on them. Talk to them while I'm making fajitas. Would you like one, or have you already eaten dinner?"

"I'll take three if you can spare that many."

"Oh, I think I'll be able to feed all of you so you don't starve."

Thank heaven she'd weathered that little squall. If Walker insisted on showing up without phoning, he was bound to meet with the unexpected. Talk about flying by the seat of his pants....

"Is Clay still on the Pedialyte?"

"He has been, but I'll put him down in a few minutes with his regular bottle. In the meantime, maybe he'll eat some Cheerios if I give them to you. I'll put a few in a plastic bag."

When she came back with them a second later, Walker had chosen one of the upholstered chairs and had settled Clay on his lap. The guys sat on the couch looking ecstatic that one of the most famous rodeo celebrities in the world was under her roof. She wouldn't put it past her brother to have purposely dropped in, hoping he'd get to meet the legendary Walker Cody.

"While I finish getting dinner ready, feel free to help yourselves to sodas or anything else you want from the fridge."

With Clay settled happily against Walker while he munched away, she got busy in the kitchen.

Within twenty minutes she called everyone to come and fix their plates before they took their food back to the living room. Walker brought up the rear, still holding Clay. The guys were still firing one question after another at him. If only he knew what this meant to her brother and Ross.

The green eyes that stared into hers held no shadows this evening, an indication he was at a low-tension level. Relieved for his sake, since he had so few moments of relative inner peace, she reached for Clay. "Okay, sweetheart. It's time to put you down. I bet you're going to love your bottle."

She grabbed it off the counter. "Say nite-nite to everyone."

Clay made an indescribable sound that caused the guys to laugh, but it was Walker's smile and kiss to his forehead that touched her. She hid her face in her boy's golden curls and left the kitchen in order to deal with her emotions.

As she passed through the living room, Clay extended his arms. "Peb—Peb—"

Walker was right behind her. "Did I hear him say what I think he said?" He scooped up the pony Clay had left on the floor and handed it to him.

Paula sent him a laughing glance. "I've been working with him."

"You've made my day, sport!" He tickled Clay, who giggled.

"See you later, everybody." Her boy was tired. She walked him to the nursery. It didn't take long to get him ready for bed and give him his medicine. When she handed him the bottle, he drank thirstily, the best of signs that he was getting better.

When she went back in the other room, the guys were still talking nonstop rodeo while they finished doing the dishes.

She found her kitchen spotless and suspected that Walker was to blame. Kip could be helpful, but she knew he probably hadn't taken the initiative and started the cleanup.

Walker's gaze darted to hers. "Jesse's competing in the local rodeo tonight to get in the extra practice. I've invited Kip and Ross to follow me over to the arena on their bikes and watch the rest of the rounds. Afterward I'll introduce them to him and some of the other contestants if they want."

Both guys looked so dazed they couldn't talk.

"I've also told them they can spend the night at my cabin. That's what the loft is for, but only if you're in agreement." He rubbed the back of his neck absently. "I'd invite you to come with us, but I know Clay needs another night in his own bed. Tomorrow morning I'll show them around the ranch, and they can ride the mechanical bull if they want."

Walker, Walker. "If they *don't* want, then their brains need to be scanned for serious abnormalities."

Kip burst into laughter. "You're sure you don't mind?"

"Of course not." In all honesty this solved a big problem for her. She had little willpower around Walker and was glad Kip and Ross were there to act as a buffer. "Clay's still recovering and I could use a good night's sleep. But come by tomorrow before you leave for Yellowstone."

"Will do." He gave her a hug and a kiss before heading for the front door. Ross came over to hug her and thank her, then followed him out.

Walker lingered until the others were gone, then cupped the back of her neck. "I saw that look of panic in your eyes," he murmured against her lips. "To ease your mind, I told them about my flashbacks and gave them the choice whether to risk it or not."

He'd misread what he'd seen. "I wasn't worried. Those two can handle anything. There's nothing my brother loves more than a challenge."

"If he's anything like you, he'll meet the test because you're the most courageous woman I've ever known, on or off the battlefield." He pressed a passionate kiss to her mouth before joining the guys, who were already revving their sport bikes.

She backed up against the closed door and buried her face in her hands. Walker was so wrong about her it was chilling.

Chapter Ten

June 9

Dr. Bader looked up. "Glad you could make it, Walker. Come on in and sit down." Walker did his bidding and handed him his art tablet. "I believe you've put on a little more weight."

"Boyd told me the same thing." His hazer ate like a horse. It was catching.

"You look good," he commented before opening the drawing pad. "Nothing's been added. You must be feeling better." He closed it again and pushed it back to Walker. "Tell me about your week. How's the rodeo going?"

"So-so. I'm not getting the speed I want yet."

"But you're working on it." Walker nodded. "Any more flashbacks since the rainstorm?"

"No."

"That's encouraging. What about your father?"

"We've more or less achieved détente, at least for the present."

"Tell me."

While Walker related what had happened at his father's office, Dr. Bader's warm brown eyes lit up. "I'm happy for you." He wrote out a prescription for his medication and handed it to him. "Now I want to know what's going on with you and Paula."

He jumped up from the chair. "I wish I knew."

"Do you still feel like you're the third party in your relationship?"

"We don't have a relationship," he bit out. "After I got home from Moab, I went over to her apartment and discovered her brother and his friend there. One thing led to another and I invited them to stay at my cabin Monday night. Yesterday when we went back to her apartment as prearranged, we found a note on the door. She'd gone to Laramie for a few days to help her friend who's moving there."

"Did she address it to you?"

"No."

"How did her brother react?"

"He was surprised, but he understood."

"And you?" Walker couldn't answer. "In other words you took it as a rejection. Why would you do that when she left a message that included everyone? Did you have definite plans with her that she broke?"

"No. Like a fool I assumed she wanted to be with me."

"Have you talked to her since?"

Walker sucked in his breath. "No."

"Why not?"

"Because I don't want to hear her give me the heave-ho."

"You think that's what she's going to do?"

"She just did it to another poor devil. It's only a matter of time."

"What aren't you telling me?"

"Nothing." He spun away and headed for the door. On the way out, he turned to him. "I don't have it in me to talk today. Sorry to have wasted your time."

"It's never a waste. You've already taken the steps to get into your career as the head of the J. W. Cody Natural Gas Company. You're doing fine, Walker. See you next week."

Doing fine when he felt gutted? *The right woman will love you, warts and all.* Sure she would.

A blackness crept over him as he sped away from the clinic.

"IT'S A GOOD THING there's only reserved seating, because this place is packed!" Angie said. Paula nodded. According to some locals sitting behind them, every night the stands were full like this all summer long. The rodeo was a different world, one she'd never had an interest in, but the advent of Walker Cody on the scene had forced her to think about it.

Tonight Angie had challenged Paula to come. At least watch Walker compete one time before she shut him out of her life. Since Paula had told Walker she would attend the rodeo on Saturday night and her friend had wanted to see it, she'd reluctantly agreed.

This was Angie's last night in Cody. Her friend had come back to finish cleaning her apartment. Tomorrow she and Danice would be leaving for good. Katy was babysitting the children at Paula's apartment.

It was one of those beautiful Wyoming June nights. The temperature was warm enough they didn't need a wrap, but Paula couldn't appreciate it. "I wish we were watching Walker do anything but this."

Angie rolled her eyes. "You mean you'd prefer to watch him fly around a track in a Formula One race car at death-defying speeds instead?"

"I meant golf or tennis. A sane sport."

"You're talking about a Cody. They settled this land. Walker's a different breed. Admit that's part of the fascination."

"I admit it, but I don't have to like the fact that he's dealing with an unpredictable animal. His father's leg was never the same again because he couldn't get away from the bull in time. I told you what happened to his sister, Elly." She didn't bring up Troy's name. She couldn't.

"Ladies and gentlemen," sounded the announcer from the buzzard's roost. "The runner-up to Miss Wyoming has just led us in the flag ceremony followed by some of the participants in tonight's events."

Paula sat up straighter. She and Angie had comfortable seating beneath the grandstand, allowing them an unobstructed view. It looked like every one of the 5,500 seats beneath the cover was taken.

"We'll now have the invocation," the announcer said.

As she closed her eyes, images of Walker flooded her mind. She knew he was across the arena behind the pens somewhere with his siblings while they prepared for tonight's competition. He hadn't called or come by since Tuesday when she wasn't there.

After the note she'd left explaining that Angie needed help with Danice while she made the move to Laramie, Paula hadn't expected to see him. It was better this way.

"Father, tonight we thank You so much for our blessings, above all the gift of freedom. For today we don't understand that the gift we enjoy was not free. The men and women who have died were sacrificed so that today we may remain free as well as protect others around this entire world."

The man's unexpected words touched Paula in the deepest part of her soul. While Brent had made the ultimate sacrifice, Walker had been able to come home. He'd been one of the lucky ones. Hadn't his war wounds taught him anything?

Angie put a comforting hand on her arm for a moment before withdrawing it.

"And Father, we ask that You watch over and protect our cowboys and cowgirls, our rodeo livestock, our rodeo fans. Keep us all free from injury and give us grace traveling home.

Forgive us for we all fall so short. We ask this above all things. Amen."

Please protect Walker. Please.

"Amen," she whispered along with the thousands of other amens. After they sang the national anthem the announcer said, "It's going to get Western in a hurry with the bareback riding!"

The cheers were deafening. Knowing the Codys were contenders in most of the events filled her with such a dichotomy of emotions, she didn't know if she could sit there much longer. This was the second night of this particular competition, and the rising tension was palpable.

Next came the barrel racing. After five contenders Ellen Cody rode out to circle the barrels with speed and grace. It was pure poetry watching her maneuver her horse. Paula leaned closer to Angie. "You would never know she had a close call at the last rodeo. They had to cart her away from the arena in an ambulance."

Her friend didn't have a comeback for that sobering piece of news.

Soon the team roping started. Ten sets of ropers competed, Dexter and Dusty Cody among them. The announcer mentioned Dusty Cody, who'd be coming up again in the tie-down roping event. Both brothers worked fast and were sensational.

Each event went so quickly, a whole evening flashed by without her realizing it. The bull riding event was next, bringing a huge roar from the crowd.

There were ten contenders, most of them wearing vests and helmets. When Jesse Cody and his bull, Foxey Loxey, were announced, the crowd went wild. His body looked fluid no matter how the bull twisted and jerked. The white cowboy hat he was wearing didn't even fall off. He received a score of ninety and the crowd jumped to their feet to cheer him.

Another local bull rider named Mark Hansen rode a bull called Rip Torn and received an eighty-nine. There were more ovations. One more competitor to go before it was Walker's event. Her heart was already jumping in her throat.

"Robby Tedesco's up next riding Tsunami. He's been having a great season. With the scores he's racked up and a good ride tonight, he could come out on top. That bull has given grief before, but Robby's staying with h— Uh-oh. He's off! He needs to get away, but he's hurt. I believe those hind legs got him in the thigh. He's clutching it. Now he's being helped out of the arena. We'll give you folks an update when one's available. Our next event is the steer wrestling."

As the crowd roared with renewed excitement, Paula jumped to her feet, feeling sick. "I can't watch any more, Angie, but you stay until it's over. I'll wait for you in my car."

"No, no. I'll come with you. I need a good night's sleep before the long drive tomorrow."

They made their way out of the stands to the parking area. Halfway home Angie broke the silence. "Don't let what happened tonight become bigger in your mind than it is, Paula. He limped out of there with help. Injuries are par for the course."

"I know. My brother's had his share, but if you could see Walker's scars, you'd understand my concern better. If one of those horns got him in the side, I don't know how the doctors would be able to fix him up."

Angie stared at her. "I can see your fear goes a lot deeper than I'd realized. I'm sorry because I think Walker's good for you."

"Let's not talk about him."

"Deal."

Paula's eyes smarted. "I didn't mean to snap at you. Forgive me. With you leaving in the morning for good, I'm afraid tonight's not my best night. You've been the best friend I ever had."

"Hey—I'm only going to Laramie."

She drove past Angie's car and pulled into her parking stall. "At the end of the semester, I'll take time off from work so we can get together with the kids. But it won't be the same as our living in the same complex, and you know it."

"I know. I'd give anything if you were moving to Laramie, too."

"You're going to become a fabulous RN and have a fabulous life with Danice. I know wonderful things are in store for you."

Now Angie teared up. "Our stories aren't written yet."

"You're right." Paula needed to get a different story going herself.

THAT NIGHT, FOR THE FIRST time in a long time, she had a horrendous nightmare. Instead of the military knocking on her door, she was sitting in an arena and the rodeo announcer said, "Ladies and gentlemen, we're canceling the rest of tonight's competition due to the tragic news that Walker Cody died on the way to the hospital."

"No!" Paula screamed in agony and bolted upright in the bed. The dream had been so real her heart thundered in her chest and she'd broken out in a cold sweat. From the nursery she could hear Clay crying. Her fright had been so terrible, she'd wakened him. A flashback couldn't have done worse damage. Her compassion for Walker knew no bounds.

She rushed to Clay's room and brought him back to bed. After she cuddled him for a long time, he fell back to sleep. Paula lay there for the rest of the night fighting her demons.

At seven-thirty while she was feeding Clay his breakfast in the high chair, her mom phoned to find out how he was doing. Pretty soon her dad got on to say hello, then Kip took over.

"Hey, Pollywog. You did a real disappearing act on Tuesday."

She lowered her head. "I know. Angie called, desperate for help because her sister in Laramie was down with the flu. She'd been counting on her."

"So it was my sister to the rescue."

"You'd do the same thing for Ross."

"Guilty as charged."

"D-did you have a good time with Walker?" she stammered.

"I don't know where to begin. Let's just say I experienced one of the greatest times of my life." He went quiet for a moment before he said, "He's...not like anyone else I've ever known."

Paula could relate. Every moment spent with Walker provided unparalleled thrills. "No. Walker Cody is unique."

"He showed us the new ranch house. You really did a fabulous job on the landscaping for them. It's a beautiful place. Incredible! I'm proud of you, Paula. The folks are proud of you, too."

"Thanks," she whispered in a shaken voice.

"Is Clay better?"

"He's fine now."

"Did you get to the rodeo last night?"

She had trouble breathing. "Yes. I went with Angie, but we couldn't stay for all of it because she was getting ready to leave for Laramie early this morning."

"But you saw Walker compete."

"Actually we left at the end of the bull riding."

"You're kidding. On the Pro Rodeo Web site it says Walker put up a 3.9. That's his best time this season."

"I'm sure that pleases him. He's been working so hard."

Kip made a funny noise in his throat. "He won't be happy until he gets a 3.3 or 3.4."

After her nightmare she didn't want to talk about it. "There's another phone call coming in. It might be a client. I've got to go."

"Okay. Talk to you later."

She hung up with him and clicked on the new caller. "Hello?"

"Paula?"

At the sound of Walker's voice she went weak and sank down on one of the kitchen chairs. "Hi."

"Hi, yourself. How's my little guy?"

Clay was playing with his cereal. "He's all better."

"I'm glad to hear it. And what about you?"

Don't ask. "I'm fine."

"No you're not. What's wrong?"

"My friend Angie left for Laramie this morning. It's a wrench for me and Clay. We've been close ever since Brent and I first moved here."

"I have a remedy for that," he informed her. "How about we spend part of the day at the folks' pool? It'll be relaxing. No one will be around. We won't let Clay get any water in his ears."

Now was the time to be strong. "That's very generous of you, but—"

"But what?" he cut in on her in a terse voice.

She got up from the chair and paced. "I don't think it would be a good idea."

"Why don't you just say it? I'm not your husband," he ground out.

Her face went hot. "You're jumping to conclusions again," she said angrily. "Brent has nothing to do with it, and don't you dare hang up on me, Walker Cody! I'm trying to explain myself and I'm not doing a very good job."

While the blood was pounding in her ears, he said, "I'll be over for you and Clay at nine. If you're not there, then we'll know if you're telling the truth or not, won't we."

The line went dead.

Paula buried her face in her hands. After sitting there for a while, she realized that she was doing to Walker what she'd accused Brent of doing to her. While he was deployed, she'd begged him to tell her what was going on in his gut, but he wouldn't, couldn't.

Now Walker wanted answers, and she was avoiding them in every way she could. She realized that after this phone call, she couldn't go on like this. It wasn't fair to either of them.

When he came for her and Clay, she'd be ready to go with him. But by the time he brought her back to the apartment, she would have granted him the favor Brent hadn't granted her.

Though it would be the kiss of death to their relationship, *gut talk* was what Walker wanted from her. That's what he'd get.

WALKER GRABBED HIS CELL phone and called Elly. Along with the rental agreement, Jesse had left him a list of the family's phone numbers. At the time Walker hadn't paid much attention, but things had changed. *He'd* changed. The next time he talked to Jesse, he would thank him for his foresight.

Come on, Elly. Pick up.

After five rings he heard her say hello.

"Elly? It's Walker."

"Hey, Walker! I can't believe you're calling me."

"I'm sure you can't. Jesse gave me your number. I hope I'm not phoning too early."

"Are you kidding? I'm about to leave the homestead to check on Pepper. She was favoring her left hind leg last night. I'm hoping she's all right. I want to take her for a ride."

"I hope so, too, because I was going to suggest we start riding in the mornings beginning tomorrow. If I get a ride in before Boyd and I put in practice every day, both my horse and I will get the workout we need."

"I'd love it. You know that."

"So would I. Tell me something. What are your plans today?"

"After my ride, nothing until Janie and I go into town for a meal later. Why?"

"I was wondering if you'd come by the pool in about an hour. I'm bringing Paula Olsen and her boy Clay with me."

"The landscape architect?"

"Yes."

"Is she…"

Walker knew what his sister was asking. It was only natural. "She lost her husband in Afghanistan and has been going to therapy at the VA clinic with me in Powell." Another slight exaggeration.

"The poor thing."

"You could say we need each other."

"I understand."

"She doesn't get much of a breather being a full-time mom. What I'm hoping is that you'd keep an eye on her cute little two-year-old for a half hour."

"Don't say another word. I'll be happy to do it."

"I'll make this up to you, Elly."

"Oh for heaven's sake—"

He smiled. "All right, here's the plan. If you could make it look like you just happened to come out to the pool and took a liking to Clay. You know, ask Paula if you could take him in the house so Mom could see him? I just need a little time alone with her."

"You can count on me."

His throat swelled. "I know. I've got a great family. See you later." Walker hung up, grateful for Elly.

Twenty minutes later he was driving to Cody. He didn't really believe Paula would run away from him this morning. Still, when he saw her at the apartment railing putting out the things Clay would need, his lungs expelled the breath he'd been holding.

"Hi!" She waved to him as if she hadn't tried to widen the distance between them. "Clay's been waiting for you."

She smelled delicious and looked incredible in a khaki wraparound skirt and a lacy, white short-sleeved jacket. He suspected she had her bathing suit on underneath.

Clay saw him coming up the stairs and reached for him.

Walker pulled the boy out of her arms and gave him a big hug. He kissed his tummy, producing belly laughter that was music to his ears. He'd missed the little guy. After they played for a minute, he transferred the car seat to his truck and they were off.

Though he'd wanted to take them to the cabin for the conversation he had in mind, he decided the ranch-house pool represented a safer, less threatening spot for Paula. Somewhere more civilized.

He turned his head toward her, marveling anew at her lovely profile. There was nothing about her he didn't like. Not until she'd tried to stop him cold over the phone. "Do you need anything from town before we drive to the ranch?"

"I don't, thank you, but if you want something, please go ahead."

"Nothing for me." He started for the outskirts. "Have you heard from Kip?"

"Yes. I talked to him this morning. My whole family in fact." Her head was bowed. "Thank you for giving him and Ross the thrill of their lives."

"That's a gross exaggeration, but I'll accept the compliment all the same. I was impressed with how experienced they are at bulldogging."

"It was Kip's dream. He told me you got a 3.9 at the rodeo last night." A band constricted her breathing. "I was there with Angie, but we had to get home to the babysitter before your event."

He shot her a sideward glance. "Was that before or after Robby Tedesco's injury?"

Her hands moved restlessly. "After."

Just as he'd thought. "In case you were wondering, he didn't break any bones, but he'll be bruised for a while."

"I'm glad it wasn't more serious than that." She was still looking out the passenger window. "Where's your next rodeo?"

"The Crazy Horse Stampede in South Dakota. I've got to take advantage of the rodeos I can, including performing most nights here in Cody until the Roundup up on the Fourth of July."

"You've set yourself a very rigorous schedule."

Yup. It's kept me from rushing you. "I have to if I'm going to get my time down."

She remained unusually quiet for the rest of the drive. He, on the other hand, kept up a conversation with Clay, who made noises now and then to let him know he was communicating the best way he could. When Walker looked back at him through the rearview mirror and Clay broke out in a smile that revealed his baby teeth, a feeling of love for the boy crept into his heart of its own volition.

HER EMOTIONS IN CHAOS, Paula followed Walker and Clay around the side of the house to the pool. Before the day was out, she would tell him she couldn't go on seeing him. After the nightmare that had taken its toll on her, she couldn't risk being involved with a man who deliberately put himself in danger.

He kept talking about the Cody Roundup, but that wouldn't be the end of it. There'd always be another rodeo stretching to infinity. That's what it felt like. She couldn't handle it.

"You can change over there in the cabana," he said in a deep, mellow voice. "I'll keep an eye on Clay."

She nodded before doing as he suggested. Inside the changing room, complete with a shower, towels and every cosmetic one could want, she undid her skirt and took off her sandals.

Wrapping one of the towels around her body, she emerged to discover Walker had removed his clothes and wore a pair of navy swim trunks that rode low on his hips. Except for the scarring, she could find no flaw in him or in his superb physique.

In a desperate attempt to quell her desire for him, she tested the water. "This is a great temperature for Clay. Let's put him on the step so he can play there for a little while." She'd already put his bathing suit on over his diaper.

Walker took him to the shallow end and got in the water. With infinite care he lowered Clay to the first step and talked to him as he gently splashed Clay a little to help him get used to it.

Her son loved water and started patting it with his hands. Soon he was kicking his sturdy legs, causing Walker to laugh out loud. His patience with her son revealed depths of his character. He genuinely enjoyed Clay.

The fun-loving part of Walker that had been buried for so many years came out when he was around her little boy. Her heart hurt to think his life experiences had been so painful, he'd almost forgotten how to be carefree.

Before she took off her towel and got in, too, she heard a female voice cry out Walker's name. Paula turned her head to see a young blonde version of Anne Cody walk out on the deck dressed in jeans and a red print top. "I thought that was your laugh and came out to investigate. I was looking for Mom and didn't think anyone else was here."

"We just arrived. Elly, meet Paula Olsen, the woman who transformed the grounds around here. And this is her son, Clay."

His sister wore her hair in a ponytail. It swished back and forth as she walked over to her. "Hi! I've always wanted to meet you. Everyone who comes to the house lavishes praise over the job you did on the landscaping."

"Thank you, Elly. It was an exciting project."

She shook her head. "To have your talent…"

"You've got a ton of your own," Walker asserted.

"I'll say you do," Paula chimed in. "I saw your performance during the barrel racing last night. You were so sensational, I was awestruck."

"Really?"

Like Walker, Elly Cody displayed a rare modesty that won Paula over.

His eyes leveled on Paula. "My sister's a fabulous photographer, too. Between her prizewinning photos and your paintings, the two of you have a lot in common. One day you'll have to get together." He got out of the pool and brought Clay over to her, but her son was preoccupied by the jade piece.

"Oh, isn't he adorable."

Paula smiled. "I think so."

"Can I hold him? Do you think he'd let me?"

"Here. Take this towel first or you'll get soaked."

"I don't mind." She wrapped it around Clay and settled him in her arms. "Oh, you're so cute I could eat you up." Clay was so distracted by all the attention, he forgot to cry. "Paula? Do you mind if I take him in the house? Mom will go crazy when she finds out who has come to visit."

"Are you sure?"

"Positive. I see you brought a baby bag. If I need anything, I'll get it out. In case you're worried, I've done my share of babysitting in my time."

"I'm not worried. He seems perfectly content to be with you right now."

"It's called the Cody Effect," Walker drawled.

Elly rolled her eyes at her brother before grabbing the bag. "Trust you to come up with that one. Are you ready, little cutie? Let's go inside. Do you like bananas? I bet there's one in the kitchen waiting for you."

Paula happened to glance at Walker. The memory of him feeding Clay a banana was on both their minds. The smile he gave her was so sweet it hurt. "Since Clay is being supervised for the moment, there's something I want to show you. Come on. We'll go in the truck. We won't be long."

"But I'm still in my suit."

"So am I."

"I'd still be more comfortable with a skirt on. Just a minute." She dashed over to the cabana and put it back on, along with her sandals. When she joined him again, he'd slipped on a T-shirt.

"After we get back, we'll swim. Your brother told me you set the lifetime best in college for the four-hundred-yard individual medley in the Western Athletic Conference Championships in Houston."

"Oh dear. I guess nothing's sacred."

"Nope."

His wicked grin told her he possessed other secrets, too.

Chapter Eleven

Walker drove them on an outer road through rangeland to a part of the Cottonwood Ranch where she'd never been. In the distance she saw a natural-gas well. After a few miles she spied another and then another. He kept driving until she couldn't see any more.

He eventually turned off the road and pulled up in front of an old line shack probably used by one of their stockmen during the winter months. She'd seen one depicted in a Charles Russell painting that looked just like it.

She flicked him a curious glance. "Why are we stopping here?"

"I thought you'd like to see my temporary office. This is where you'll find me when I get a moment."

"This shack?"

His eyes lit up with an excitement she'd never seen before. "You're the first person to behold the future J. W. Cody Natural Gas Company."

Paula stirred restlessly in her seat, wondering if she'd heard him correctly. "I thought you told me you leased this part of your land to the Spurling Natural Gas Company."

"We do, but that will come to an end next year."

"I don't understand."

For the next few minutes he explained about the conversation with his father. He not only gave her the history behind the natural-gas field on their property, but he told her his hopes of finding another one north of where they were parked and that he was going to fund it himself. "I came up with this idea before I graduated from the University of Montana."

"You went to Missoula?" Everything he told her was a revelation.

He nodded.

"But then how did you manage to be that far away from the ranch and still be on the rodeo circuit?"

"It wasn't easy. Every minute had to count."

Not easy? she cried inwardly. He had to be some kind of genius to balance school and rodeo and still win a world rodeo championship. There were more facets to Walker Cody than she would ever have imagined.

"Hey." He leaned across and cupped her chin in his hand. "You're not saying anything. What do you think about my plan?"

What did she think? He'd thrown so much at her all at once, she was spinning. For sure he was the greatest risk taker she'd ever known.

"I think you're a throwback to your ancestor whose picture is hanging in the ranch office. He was a visionary man, too."

Walker pressed a kiss to the side of her mouth before sitting back. His touch sent fingers of delight through her sensitized body. "Let's hope my vision produces his kind of results."

She had no doubts it would, provided he lived long enough to see it become a reality. "Is your father behind you in this?" she asked quietly.

"All the way." She heard satisfaction in his voice. It appeared that whatever issues he'd had with J.W., he'd gotten past them.

"You're surprised, aren't you?"

"I suppose I am," she answered softly, "but it's none of my business."

"Then I'm going to make it your business so you'll understand. My siblings never seemed to have much trouble with my father, but I always did because we're so different. Still, life went on the same until my senior year in high school when I was upset with him for trying to keep me from going to the prom. He had other ideas about me doing a competition that night.

"Troy and I took off and that's when he told me something about my father that hit me so hard, I lost my natural affection for him."

As Paula listened, her pain for Walker grew. If she'd been his age when she'd learned that her father had carried on an affair with another woman early in her parents' marriage, it would have been so devastating, she couldn't imagine getting over it.

"The anger I felt stayed bottled up inside me throughout college and my years in the service. When I saw Mother for the first time after coming back from Iraq, she wanted to know why I resented Dad. At that point I asked her if the rumor was true. She didn't deny it.

"I'm afraid my disgust with him came out in my artwork. Dr. Bader picked up on it and we had a talk. To make a long story short, he informed me the war hadn't done near the damage to me I'd done to myself by not forgiving my father, who, he reminded me, wasn't a perfect man. Nor was I.

"By staying away from the rodeo, I thought I was punishing him, but all I'd managed to do was keep myself away from a sport I loved, and separate myself from my siblings, which caused grief for them and unnecessary guilt for me."

"Dr. Bader's a brilliant man."

"I agree. After his talk sank in, I realized Mom must have forgiven Dad, so why couldn't I? Unless Mom has told him, he doesn't know that I know. I'm still working on building a new relationship with him, but things are better between us."

"They must be or he wouldn't willingly turn over part of the Cody empire to you. It's wonderful news." She was thrilled for him. Averting her eyes she said, "So you're going to start a new company and still compete in the rodeo?" It was a rhetorical question because she already knew the answer.

"Of course."

Of course. He was only twenty-eight. He had several years yet to be at the top of his form, like Jesse. "I think we'd better go back. I'm sure your sister didn't expect to find us gone. If Clay's missing me, he can be a handful."

Walker slid a strong hand to her thigh and squeezed it before starting up the truck and turning around. The contact rocked her whole body. When they'd first left the ranch house, she'd thought he was going to take her someplace private where she'd lose control in his arms, the one thing she couldn't afford to do.

Surprise, surprise.

What Paula needed to do was get a life for herself beyond her work. With Angie gone from Cody, maybe it was time for her to do the same....

If she were to move back to Rexburg, a city of eighteen thousand, she could buy a little house and be a landscape architect there. Her family would be overjoyed and Clay would thrive. She'd work things out so Clay saw his other grandparents.

The move would give her new opportunities to meet people. As Angie had said, it was time to leave herself open to new possibilities. When she got back home today, she'd make housing and job inquiries. With her portfolio, she had every reason to be optimistic.

Naturally there would never be another tall, dark and dangerous man like Walker Cody, but the nightmare last night had proved she couldn't go on this way any longer. Living with fear was no way to live. By the time they reached the parking area at the ranch house, she'd determined to tell Walker the truth while they were in the pool.

He turned his head toward her. "I need to phone Boyd and let him know my plans. I'll join you and Clay in a minute."

"That's fine." She got out of the truck and hurried to the back of the house. Elly was walking Clay around the pool. They were both so blond, they could be mother and son.

Paula waved to them. "Sorry we were so long."

"No problem. Mom wasn't here so we just explored the house and then came outside."

Clay saw her and started running toward her as fast as his sturdy legs could go calling "ma ma." For the first time the sounds were distinct. She grabbed him and swung him around before hugging him again in delight. "How's my boy? Did you wonder where I'd gone?" After kissing him, she looked at Elly over his curls. "Did he cry a lot?"

"No. He was terrific and ate all the food you packed for him. If you want to know the truth, I'd like to steal him."

"Thank you for watching him. I know it wasn't on your schedule for today. I feel like I should pay you."

"Don't be silly. It was a pleasure. One day I'd give anything to have a cute little boy like him." While they were talking, Walker suddenly appeared. Instead of coming over to them, he took off his shirt and dived in the water.

"I'm sure you will," Paula said. Seeing his lean body almost made her lose her train of thought.

"With zero marriages in this family so far, it's doubtful," Elly quipped with a smile. Since danger was the middle name of the attractive Cody siblings, they found the rodeo far too fascinating to settle down to anything as mundane as marriage. The sooner she removed herself from Walker's sphere, the better.

"Thanks again. I guess Clay and I had better join your brother."

Elly rolled her eyes once more. "Good idea or he'll show no mercy and throw you in the deep end of the pool. Then it's everyone swim for your lives!" Paula laughed, but inside, the idea of swimming for her life with Walker in pursuit left her breathless.

"Come on in!" he called to her as she walked Clay across the patio. He was treading water at the far end of the pool as if he were lying in wait. Elly's comment of a moment ago didn't seem so far-fetched.

Paula struggled to keep her composure before putting Clay in his swing so he could watch them. Once more she entered the cabana and took off her clothes. Underneath she was wearing a new, white, two-piece bathing suit.

When she swam for the university, they'd all worn one-piece suits. It had never bothered her to walk in front of hundreds of spectators, but knowing Walker was out there and would be watching sent her into a panic. Without a tan, white did little for her, but it had been the most modest suit she could find.

Having a baby had added to her curves. She needed to get on a disciplined swimming regimen to tone her body. It would probably never perform the way it once did, and she shouldn't be worrying about that now, but she couldn't help it because—because she wanted to look good for the man outside.

"Paula? Is anything wrong?"

"No! I'm coming!" She swallowed hard and headed out the door to discover Walker had gotten out of the pool and was hunkered down next to Clay, swinging him back and forth.

He turned his head when he saw her. She felt his gaze sweep over her in intimate appraisal. It caused her body to break out in heat. Walking to the end of the pool, she dived in and did five laps before surfacing. By now Walker was in the water. He swam over to her, then tossed his head back. She'd never seen his eyes so alive.

"Last one to the other end will have to pay a penalty. Are you game?"

"Are you?" she challenged. No one ever bested him at anything, but she was going to try.

"Do you need to catch your breath first?" Wouldn't he love it if she said yes.

"No."

A devilish sound escaped his throat. "On three, then." He gave the countdown and they were off. As they cleaved the water side by side, her excitement grew. She thought they were matching stroke for stroke. At the other end their heads lifted at the exact same time.

"It was a draw!" she cried, gleeful that he hadn't beaten her the first time out.

His expression didn't look quite as triumphant as before. "We'll do it again," he muttered.

"You're on. I'll count. One, two, three!"

Their second round went the same as before with both of them surfacing together. Trying to keep from grinning, she said, "Shall we go for one more?"

Walker's handsome features had hardened. The true competitor was revealed at last. "I'm ready if you are. I'll count, and this time I won't give you the edge," he announced in a no-nonsense tone.

"Hah!" At the sound of three she went deep and did the first part underwater to prevent drag. Using her feet in the dolphin kick, she undulated them and her body and came out first on the other end. Walker arrived a close second.

He grabbed her around the waist as she was trying to get out to reach Clay. "That was an incredible stunt you just pulled," he murmured, drawing her close against his hard-muscled body. "I feel sorry for your competitors."

"What I did wasn't any different than the way you master leverage to bring down a steer faster than anyone else."

The fire in his eyes whipped up a storm inside her. "Don't I wish. Go ahead and give me any penalty you can think of."

"I'm trying to think of a good one," she teased. They were both out of breath.

"If you haven't got any ideas, I have the only one that matters." His mouth descended, kissing her with an urgency and passion his earlier kisses had only hinted at.

This was a man's kiss, hot with desire for which she had no defense.

With their bodies and legs molded to each other, rapture spiraled through her, blotting out time, space, identity, will. In this man's arms, she could say goodbye to all of it. Finally he allowed her a breath of air.

"That wasn't a penalty," she whispered shakily. "Y-you weren't supposed to like it."

"It's too late to come up with anything else now." Cutting off her escape route, he drank deeply from her mouth again until they were giving kiss for kiss, each one hungrier and more intense than the last.

As she moaned her need of him, there was a tremendous crack of sound in the atmosphere, louder than thunder at this elevation. When she could gather her wits she realized it was a jet overhead that had just broken the sound barrier. Clay burst into tears.

"Incoming!" Walker shouted. His body hardened to steel. In the next instant, he covered her head with his arms and pressed her so hard against his chest she couldn't breathe.

Worse, her mouth was just below the water, but his hold on her was like a vise.

He was back in Iraq!

Don't panic, Paula.

Her son cried harder.

"Don't die, don't die…" She heard Walker's mantra.

As he turned both their bodies toward the sound of Clay's voice, the corner of her jaw took a hit against the edge of the pool, but it allowed her to drink in gulps of air. Using uncommon strength she caught his face in her hands and forced it upward. He'd gone pale and his eyes were glazed, exactly as they'd been at the parade.

"Walker? It's Paula. You're not in Iraq. We're in the pool at the ranch house. We're all fine. Clay's fine. Can you hear me?"

She watched his hand reach for the jade and press it. "I'm not in Iraq." He repeated the words like a litany.

"No, you're not in Iraq. You're here safe with me." She wrapped her arms around his waist and burrowed her face in his neck. "You're all right. Everyone's fine," she said over and over again in a soothing tone until she felt his rigid body start to relax.

"Paula?" he whispered. When she lifted her head, she was thankful to see recognition in his eyes once more. Clay was in hysterics, but it was more important she soothe Walker first.

"You're bleeding!" He sounded horrified.

"It's nothing. I scraped the edge of the pool by accident."

He took a shuddering breath. "What's wrong with Clay?"

"Nothing serious. He got upset when a jet overhead broke the sound barrier. Come on. Let's get out of the pool." As they used the steps to reach the deck, she could feel his body trembling.

"I'm coming, sweetheart." Grabbing a towel, she pressed it to her chin, then hurried over and pulled him out of his swing. "Did that big plane scare you?"

Walker was right behind her and put his arms around both of them. "What have I done to you?" The sorrow in his voice just about killed her.

"You haven't done anything. See? Clay's already settling down and wants you to hold him."

Once the boy was in his arms she heard Walker say, "I love you, sport." He walked around the patio with her son to comfort him. Paula took advantage of the time to wash her hair and shower in the cabana before getting dressed. When she came out, Walker had put Clay on his lap so he could drink his bottle.

He watched her approach him. "I'll drive you home. Just give me a few minutes to get showered and dressed first."

"Take all the time you need." She plucked Clay from his arms and sat down in one of the deck chairs while he finished his bottle.

Walker surprised her when a short time later he appeared from the cabana showered and dressed, carrying a first-aid kit. "We need to take care of that cut."

"It stopped bleeding right away and isn't deep."

"Nevertheless it needs attention until a doctor can look at it. Put your head back."

Paula did his bidding while he wiped the wound with an antiseptic pad and put a small bandage over it. He did his job with the expertise of a medic in the field. She couldn't help but wonder how many of the men under his command had been the recipient of his services in combat.

He left the kit on the table. "Let's go." With the swing in one arm and the baby bag in the other, he walked them around the side of the house to the truck. Once settled in the cab, he turned to her.

"I'd planned for us to eat lunch here, but I think Clay's had enough upset for one day. We'll pick up some hamburgers in town and take them to your apartment."

She nodded, glad he'd made that suggestion because food was the last thing on her mind right now.

"But first we'll stop by the E.R. and have them take a look at that cut."

"You really think it's necessary?"

His lips tightened. "I think it needs a couple of stitches."

"All right."

An hour and a half later Walker helped her and Clay in the apartment. Sure enough she'd needed two stitches. He insisted on doing everything, including putting Clay down. A few minutes later he joined her in the kitchen and sat down in one of the other chairs next to her, but he didn't touch his food. She saw the anxiety in his eyes.

"How are you feeling?"

"I'm fine."

"No, you're not."

"Hey…" She smiled at him, wishing she had the power to take his worry away. "Now I have a mark of bravery from the war, too."

He seemed to have trouble swallowing. "Don't joke about this. It's too serious."

"The only thing serious is your overreaction to one tiny cut." She put down the last of her hamburger. "You were trying to protect me and turned us both against the side of the pool for a shield. If there'd been a bomb, you'd have gotten the worst of it, not me."

She heard his sharp intake of breath. "I'm no good for you."

Her stomach twisted when he said things like that. "This

has gone far enough, Walker. You're using your PTSD as an excuse for what's really wrong. For heaven's sake, tell me what's going on inside you. You're as closemouthed as Brent!"

Lines marred his striking features. "I guess I should be flattered you could come up with a comparison."

While she was trying to figure out what that was supposed to mean, he sprang to his feet. "I've got to go."

Now he'd made her angry. "You *always* have to go."

"Yup."

As he turned away from her she glimpsed panic in his eyes. "Wait—" She raced after him, but he was already out the front door and down the stairs. She moved fast, but she couldn't catch up to him.

By the time she reached the lower level in front of Angie's vacant apartment, his truck had disappeared. In the distance she heard the squeal of tires. It sounded as if he was running for his life.

Her hands curled into fists. How easy for him to take off when he knew she couldn't leave Clay to follow him.

Run then, Walker Cody! It's better this way. You've just saved me the trouble of having to tell you your world is too dangerous for me.

"LADIES AND GENTLEMEN, you just saw Walker Cody from Markton, Wyoming, clock a time of 4.2 this round. After the momentum he got at the Cody Rodeo in Wyoming last weekend, this has to be a bit of a disappointment for him here at the Crazy Horse Stampede. Wylie Hodges, number two in the world standings from Austin, Texas, is in the box now. He—"

Walker didn't wait to hear any more. He exited the arena where Jesse was waiting for him behind the barrier. Boyd indicated he'd take care of Peaches.

He eyed his brother. "Who am I kidding, Jesse? My timing's off. I haven't got it."

"We all have our bad nights. I had a bad one myself tonight."

At least Mark Hansen hadn't come to South Dakota to compete in this one. That had to be a plus for Jesse. "An eighty-eight is in the ballpark, bro." They walked out behind the pens. "With a 4.2, I might as well chuck it all in. Six years away have taken their toll."

Jesse squinted at him out of those brilliant blue eyes. "That's not the reason. Don't you think it's time we discussed Paula Olsen?"

His jaw hardened. "Who's been talking?"

"Who hasn't?"

"Hell."

"Don't you know there aren't any secrets on the Cottonwood Ranch? Mrs. Olsen isn't just any woman, you know."

"That's right. She's Brent Olsen's wife!"

"Ah."

Walker frowned. "What do you mean 'Ah'?" No one could get to him like his older brother.

Jesse clapped him on the shoulder. "You're the brainy one in the family. Just don't take too long figuring it out. We've got the Mesquite Championship in Dallas next weekend." He put his cowboy hat back on. "The twins are waiting at the trailer for me. They had a good night."

"I know. Tell them I'm proud of them."

He nodded. "We're going to head out now."

"Boyd and I are, too."

"See you back at the ranch."

They both took off. He loved Jesse, but little did his brother know Walker's problem was insurmountable.

THE CALL FROM ANGIE CAME after ten on Friday night when Paula was in bed. Her friend's nursing hours dictated when they could talk, but Paula would have waited for it all night if she had to. She needed to unload to her before she went crazy.

"I got your message earlier, but I couldn't call until now."

"You think I don't understand? You're a friend in a million, Angie."

"Ditto."

"How are things going?"

"Good. Danice likes the woman I found to babysit her. My sister spells her off when she can. It's saving my life."

"I know it's hard leaving Danice, but you only have four semesters to go, and then you're done."

"Oh, Paula. I was a fool to quit nursing school to get married, but then—"

"Then you wouldn't have your adorable daughter," Paula broke in. "So you can't think that way."

"You're right. How's my favorite little boy?"

"He's good. I know he's missing Danice. Whenever we go down the stairs, he wants to run into your apartment and looks up at me in such bewilderment." She knew Clay was wondering where Walker was, too.

Angie sniffed. "You shouldn't have told me that. I take it you haven't heard from Walker since we talked the other day."

"No. It's been two weeks since he did his disappearing act. No phone calls. Nothing."

"Considering the extent of your fear, it's probably best that it ended this way."

Paula's heart started to race. "That's what I wanted to talk to you about. I've decided I don't want it to end."

There was a long silence. "Since when?"

She jackknifed into a sitting position. "Since the time you made the remark that you didn't realize my fear was so deep-seated. I've done a lot of thinking about that. When I met Brent, he told me he was in the Reserves. The possibility that he'd have to go overseas was a given, yet I continued to date him without worrying that he'd lose his life in war.

"When Kip went through that period where he did his bulldogging, I didn't agonize that he'd be fatally injured. The thought didn't enter my mind. Only since Brent's death have I developed this…phobia."

"I'm impressed you've figured that out, Paula. It *is* a phobia, but one you came by legitimately."

"If Walker and I are ever to have a relationship, I've got to get over it."

"Agreed."

"Looking back, I can see I overreacted the day that dog tried to bite Clay."

"Maybe a little, but aren't you glad you did? Otherwise you wouldn't have gotten to know Walker."

The thought of Walker not being in her life anymore was beyond her comprehension. She slid out of bed. "He thinks I'll never get over Brent, but he's wrong!"

"You and I both know that."

"His mom once told me she hoped he would start believing in himself. I don't know if he told her he might be sterile, and that was what she was talking about."

"Considering he's a Cody who's used to being the best in the world at what he does, it could be harder on him than some men."

"That's what I've been thinking. Angie? I've put a plan in action to talk to him, but I want your opinion before I carry it out."

"This is exciting. I'm all ears."

"My brother keeps me filled in on the Pro Rodeo schedules. Walker's competing at the Mesquite Championship in Dallas this weekend. In anticipation of flying down there tomorrow, I drove Clay to Garland this evening. His grandparents are going to keep him until Sunday."

"It sounds great so far. Do you know where Walker's staying?"

"When Kip was at the Cottonwood Ranch, Walker showed him and Ross around. They got to see inside his luxury horse trailer. According to Kip the interior is like a holiday villa with every amenity. Apparently Walker and Boyd stay in it on the grounds of the arenas where they compete. I won't have any problem finding it."

"Well then, I say, go for it, girl!"

AFTER A 3.7 AND A 3.6 FOR the past two nights, a dispirited Walker had to face the possibility that he was finished. Washed up.

He took care of his horse, then walked around to the living quarters of the trailer and went inside. Boyd had gone off with the guys, which was a good thing. They'd decided not to leave Dallas for the ranch until morning.

What Walker needed first was a shower to wash off the grime and sweat of the day. A few minutes later he shrugged into his robe and walked in the kitchen barefoot. Usually a hot shower helped him relax enough so he could eat, but tonight his thoughts were too black. He hadn't bothered to shave and had no appetite.

Two weeks without seeing or talking to Paula—not knowing how she was—had ruined his focus. He was torn up inside. In that amount of time Clay would already have grown so much, Walker wouldn't even recognize him. Worse, the little guy wouldn't have a clue who he was if he ever saw him again.

In an unprecedented move since returning from Iraq, he reached for the Jack Daniel's that Boyd kept on hand and poured himself a drink. A couple of them ought to send him into oblivion where he wanted to go—for tonight at least.

As he raised the glass to his lips, someone knocked on the trailer door. He was in no mood for company and took a swallow. If he ignored them, whoever it was would go away.

To his irritation they knocked again, louder this time. What the hell? He slammed the glass down on the counter spilling it and headed for the door. Whoever it was, he'd get rid of them in a hurry.

"Paula," he whispered in absolute shock after he'd flung the door open. Her fragrance assailed him.

The light from the interior illuminated her glorious blond hair and blue eyes. The sight of her standing there in designer jeans covering womanly hips and a short-sleeved denim top that cinched in at the waist rocked him back on his heels.

"I've never seen you ride before, Mr. Cody. You were awesome out there tonight."

Walker's respiration had started acting up, so he couldn't take anything more than a few shallow breaths. "What are you doing here?"

She flashed him a provocative smile. "What do *you* think?"

He held on to the door for support, not able to think. "Where's Clay?"

"With his grandparents in Garland."

Walker shook his head to clear it. Maybe he was hallucinating. "How did you get here?"

"I flew to Dallas and rented a car." He could see it behind her. "Kip gave me your rodeo schedule and described your trailer to me. The rest…was easy. Aren't you going to invite me in, or have I come at an inconvenient time?"

His emotions were in chaos. "You shouldn't be here."

She studied his taut features. "If there's a woman with you, just tell me and I'll go away, but I won't be happy about it."

Paula, Paula. "There's no one but me."

"I can smell alcohol. It's clear you're in need of help. It's group-therapy time. You and me."

"I'm afraid that isn't what I require."

"Then invite me in and we'll talk about what you *do* require."

The tiny scar on her jaw was healing. In fact it was scarcely noticeable, but he was the reason it was there at all. He closed his eyes to shut out the heavenly vision before him. "I can't do that."

"*Can't* isn't a word in my vocabulary. As I see it, you're afraid of commitment."

"Paula—"

"No, no, no. Don't interrupt. The Cody brothers are famous for not sticking to one female too long. Even Elly agrees."

He sucked in his breath. "Your opinion of us is very flattering."

She broke into a smile. "The truth scares you, doesn't it? Well, guess what, I've had some fears of my own about what could happen to you in the arena, but I'm working on them because you're worth it. There's only one way to say this. I'm in love with you, Walker, warts and all." She placed a hand on his chest, right over his heart. "Are you listening? I love *you*. Only you."

He couldn't believe what he was hearing.

"I'll always love Brent, of course. He'll have a permanent place in my heart, but he left this world a while ago. We did have one talk before he was deployed about what would happen if he never came back. He made me promise to get on with living, raise our son and find another man to love.

"When I promised him, I didn't understand what rivers of sorrow I would have to wade through. It's true that there's no one like Brent. There never will be. He's the love of my past life."

Her blue eyes welled with tears. "I'm here tonight to tell you the door to the past has closed. Another door was literally flung open when Walker Cody blazed into my life one wonderful May morning. You arrived like a bolt of lightning. The air sizzled and crackled around me, lifting the hairs on my neck. I haven't been the same since.

"The fact is, I'm so deeply in love with you, I'm afraid it's a lifetime condition. If that scares you silly, I'm not going to apologize for it. You're the great love of my new life. Got that? See you at the Roundup!" With that she walked to her car and drove off.

Walker stood in the doorway of his trailer, his mouth hanging open and his heart pounding.

Chapter Twelve

Paula kissed Clay, who was still in his high chair eating. She turned to Katy. "Thanks for being willing to babysit tonight. I don't know how soon Kip and I will be home from the Roundup, but we'll try not to be late."

"Hey, don't worry. Angie phoned and told me this is the big night for Walker Cody."

"It is."

After baring her soul to Walker outside his trailer door, he'd let her drive away in the rental car without trying to detain her. Since flying back to Cody, another whole week had gone by without a word from him. The buildup to tonight had left her nerves in such a ragged state she could hardly function. Right now her brother was the glue holding her together.

"Stay out as late as you want, Paula. I'll keep my fingers crossed for him."

"Thanks, Katy." She gave her a hug then flew out the door to join Kip, who was going to drive them to the arena in his car. He'd come on Thursday to watch the nightly competitions with her.

Every time Paula had heard Walker's name and watched him enter the box, her stomach turned over as if she were seeing him compete for the first time. To her joy, he'd gotten a 3.6 and a 3.5. Those were better scores than the ones in Mesquite.

Together, she and Kip made their way from the parking area to the covered stand, which was packed to overflowing with the Fourth of July crowd. Once they were seated, the evening got underway.

"Ladies and gentlemen, please greet Miss Wyoming and the contestants for tonight's events."

While the crowd went crazy cheering, Paula's throat swelled to see the Cody siblings ride five across. Talk about magnificent.

"Isn't that a beautiful sight? Where else on God's green earth will you see five champions from one family all together. Let's give a big hand to our own Codys from the Cottonwood Ranch!"

Paula clapped harder than anyone else. After the invocation and national anthem, the field was cleared so the events could start. An hour later it was announced the steer wrestling would be coming up next.

Kip flung an arm around Paula's shoulder. "Take it easy."

"I can't. This will be the last round for Walker. He's going to have to get a really low score to win."

"I'm betting on him. He's been shaving off time since Mesquite. I do believe your unexpected visit brought him luck."

If only that were true…

The crowd at the Cody arena pulsated with excitement. The Fourth was *the* big night in Wyoming for the rodeo fans because their own former legendary champion, Walker Cody, was in contention.

He'd brought fame to the state, not to mention to the towns of Markton and Cody. The whole region had turned out to see if he could pull off the impossible after being away from the sport for six years. Publicity for the Roundup had brought sportscasters and celebrities from all over the country.

"Ladies and gentlemen, it's time for the final round in the steer-wrestling competition."

Kip had brought his binoculars. "Here. Use these."

"Thanks." She put them to her eyes.

"You know when guys like Jimmy Hart are back in there, you can hear the silence down here. He's done really good bulldogging this week, but he's late tonight. Here's where the horse pays off. Oh, no—"

Paula watched as the steer broke loose from his grasp. By the time he got him down again, he'd run up too many seconds on the clock to be in contention.

"Here comes reigning world champion Bobby Rich, getting down on a hard-running steer. Pulls him up and throws him nice. Excellent run by Rich. 3.6. It'll be hard for anyone to beat that.

"Brad Ryder, national finalist last year from Oklahoma is out of the box next. Nice high horns. Got a 3.9 on him last night. Look at that steer. Almost threw itself down. Brad has equaled Rich's time of 3.6."

"When is it going to be Walker's turn?"

"I don't know," Kip muttered, "but it can't be too much longer now."

"Last night steer wrestlers were dropping like flies out of the competition for the big dollars. Only three men have times on all eight of their steers and are under forty seconds for all of them.

"Here goes one of them. Wylie Hodges of Austin, Texas. Great speed. Uh-oh. That steer won't go down. Uh-oh. He's running him all over the place."

Paula was getting so nervous, she was scarcely cognizant

of the next two bulldoggers. All she knew was, the time to beat was still a 3.6.

"Wyoming's own Walker Cody from the Cottonwood Ranch has entered the box."

At the sound of his name, her heart thumped unmercifully. "I think I'm going to be sick." Her admission prompted another hug from Kip. With trembling hands she studied Walker through the field glasses.

Beneath the black Stetson, his handsome facial features wore a resolute expression. To her mind his lean, powerful body looked relaxed in the saddle. He'd gained more weight. There was little resemblance to the war vet of two months ago. She saw his hand go to the charm for a second. Even from this distance she could feel his confidence.

Once the barriers opened, Peaches flew out of the box. The roar from the fans was deafening.

"Will you look at that, folks? He threw the same ornery steer that kept its head down last night. A bulldogger who knows that trick can use it to get more speed and that's what he did. A 3.3! Ladies and gentlemen, you have tonight's champion, Walker Cody, who has set a record in this arena slick as a whistle!"

The crowd went crazy and got to its feet, but no one was more hysterically happy than Paula. Tears of joy streamed down her cheeks. She hugged her brother. "He did it, Kip. He did it!"

Kip was equally dazed. "I saw it, and I still don't believe that time. Come on. Let's go find him behind the arena and congratulate him."

She shook her head. Paula didn't know what kind of a reception she would get and didn't want to find out. "He's going to be mobbed by family and friends, not to mention the media. You go. I'll wait for you in the car." She followed him to the aisle, and they slowly made their way to the outside of the grandstand. "Tell him we're both very proud of him."

He eyed her with compassion. "I will."

Tears smarted her eyes as she got in the passenger seat of Kip's car. With a time like that, Walker had to be convinced he could win a second world title in December if he stayed on the rodeo circuit. Six years away hadn't taken the bulldogger out of him.

This had to be a healing night for Walker and his father. Though he would go through the rest of his life with his soldier's wounds, he was back in the bosom of his family now, doing what he loved most.

She knew tonight's victory was particularly sweet because of Walker's ability to get past his troubles with his dad, not to mention Troy's death. In a way she sensed the rodeo had brought redemption to his soul. He *had* to be more at peace now.

Paula had never been less at peace, but knew it was essential to happiness. After risking everything last weekend when she flew down to Dallas to see him, it was a waiting game for her now.

"Hi." Kip slid behind the wheel. "Sorry I was so long. I couldn't get near Walker, but he saw me and waved." After starting the car, they made their way out of the parking area.

"Did he look happy?" Her voice throbbed.

"Oh yeah, but he was being interviewed by a couple of journalists. You know how that goes. I talked to Boyd for a minute. The Codys are having a big victory celebration at their ranch house. Only VIPs are invited."

That excluded Paula. She felt her heart die a second time.

When they reached the apartment, Katy's face was wreathed in a smile. "It was on the ten o'clock news tonight about Walker Cody. They showed a clip of him flipping that steer. He's one hot guy," she whispered to Paula.

She nodded. That said it all. "How was Clay tonight?"

"Great!"

"That's good." Paula reached in her purse to pay her. "I've added a little bonus to thank you for helping me this week."

"Thanks for the extra money. You don't know how much I need it." They hugged before she went out the door to her car.

After checking on Clay, she felt at loose ends and wandered into the dining room, where she'd left the finished watercolor on the table. It was a joyous memory of that day at the cabin with Walker.

Kip peered over her shoulder. "I think that's the best thing you've ever done."

"Really?"

"You've captured the glory of the scarlet paintbrush in the meadow outside his cabin. It's exactly the way it looks when you're sitting at the picnic table. I like the touch of the window in there. You must have been there on a perfect day for this painting to look so alive."

Her throat closed up. "It *was* a perfect day...." she whispered.

"Why didn't you enter it in that Rendezvous Royale Arts competition here? You'd have won top prize."

"Thank you for the compliment, brother dear. I considered it, but with Angie moving, a-and my life in turmoil," she stuttered, "I just didn't get around to it."

He squeezed her shoulder. "I'm going to get ready for bed. I've got a big drive ahead of me in the morning."

"I'm headed to bed myself." She checked her answering machine before turning out the lights in the kitchen and dining room.

While her brother was in the bathroom, she made up the hide-a-bed in the living room. As she was getting him an extra pillow from the linen closet, she heard a rapping on the front door. Her heart leaped because it had Walker's unmistakable cadence.

On shaky legs she opened it, then hugged the pillow to her chest to see him standing there bigger than life in his fancy Western attire and Stetson. The mysterious glimmer in those green eyes sent a current of electricity through her body.

"Walker…" She was so stunned to see him, she couldn't articulate anything else.

"That's my name," he responded in his deep voice. "I'm glad you haven't forgotten it."

She struggled for words. "You were fabulous out there tonight. I'm so proud of you."

He cocked his head. "As you can see, I'm still in one piece."

"Oh, I can see that all right," she blurted. "How did you do it? Where did you find that part inside you that made the difference?"

"It was hanging around my neck. My lucky piece. I pressed it and said to myself, I'm not in Iraq. I'm in Cody. Paula Olsen loves me, and I'm going to put that steer down faster than anyone else."

In the next breath he slid his hands up her arms to her shoulders and pulled her close while unconsciously kneading them. The contact sent a river of warmth through her veins. "Did you really mean it?"

"How can you even ask me that?" she said in raw pain.

She heard his sharp intake of breath before he looked over her shoulder. "Hey, Kip. Mind if I steal your sister for a little while?"

"How long is a little while?"

"That all depends."

"Sure. Clay and I will manage."

"Thanks." He tossed the pillow she was clutching on the couch. "Let's go." Walker grasped her hand and led her down the stairs.

"Wait—I don't even have my purse."

"You don't need it." He helped her in his truck, then started it up as if he were in a tremendous hurry.

"Where are we going?"

"To the house."

"Kip told me your parents are having a party for you."

"That's right. I told them I'd be back after I picked you up."

"You shouldn't have left. This is a huge night for you."

"That's the reason I want you with me. I can't very well announce that we're getting married if you're not there. They've already given you their seal of approval. It happened long before you came into my life like a miracle."

The world reeled as he pulled over to the side of the street and drew her into his arms. "I'm so in love with you, I can't live another second without you in my life permanently. You *are* going to marry me, aren't you?"

She saw the tiniest hint of vulnerability lingering in his eyes. "What do *you* think?"

"I think I can't make you my wife soon enough," he said in a husky tone. "We'll fly out to Reno tonight and say our vows, then come back tomorrow so Clay won't miss us too much."

"Tonight?" Her voice shook with joy.

He nodded. "After the party." In astonishment she watched him pull a ring out of the pocket of his Western shirt. "It has to be tonight because I intend to make love to you and I refuse to do that until you're Mrs. Walker Cody."

In the next breath, he slid the diamond solitaire onto her ring finger. It was a perfect fit. "Kip helped me with the sizing, by the way." When he lifted his dark head, she saw devilment in his eyes.

"What else did he do?"

The corner of his seductive mouth lifted. "That's a secret between brothers-in-law. Just so you know, I've already asked for your parents' permission to marry you, and by some miracle they said yes, provided you can put up with me. Kip vouched for me. He also packed a bag for you," he admitted before pressing a deep kiss to her mouth. "Your purse will be inside it."

"I can't believe this is really happening."

"Maybe by the time you're my wife and we're alone in bed tonight, you'll start to believe it."

She threw her arms around his neck. "I love you more than you'll ever know."

Paula couldn't stop covering his face with kisses. "You're life to me, darling."

His mouth found hers and swept her away. When he finally relinquished her mouth, he whispered, "I guess you know I worship the ground you walk on. The selfish part of me hated it that you loved Brent before you loved me. I wanted to be the only one in your life. That's why I left your apartment a couple of weeks ago."

"I know."

"But then you cleared it all up for me when you flew down to Dallas. It took me a few days to sort everything out. I just want you to know, I'm not jealous of Brent anymore."

"Thank heaven. Kiss me again and never stop. Then I'll believe it."

"Can't do that until we're alone with no deadlines except to make each other deliriously happy." In typical self-disciplined Walker Cody form, he moved away and started the truck.

"You already do that," she said with her heart in her eyes.

He grasped her hand and twined his fingers through hers. "There are degrees of happiness. We haven't begun to explore them." He kissed her fingertips. "This is going to be forever, Paula."

"I couldn't go on living if it weren't."

"I love your son as if he were my own."

"He loves you."

"I promise to do everything in my power to make certain Brent stays alive in his heart."

She studied her rodeo warrior as she thought of him. "I know you will."

"I'd love to give you more children."

"Maybe it will happen. When you're ready, I'll go with you for tests to see if there's a chance." She'd do whatever it took for him to have the experience of being a father to his own baby. "But we won't worry about it. To have your baby would be a great blessing, but it's enough that we've found each other."

"Paula…" She heard tears in his voice.

"Clay's a handful as it is. Being around the Codys will guarantee his love of the rodeo. And since you're his hero already, I can predict he'll want to be a bulldogger."

"You would approve?"

"Yes," she answered honestly. "It will be the most natural thing in the world with a father like you."

By now they'd reached the ranch. Once Walker had shut off the motor, they'd gotten so tangled in each other's arms, they were oblivious to anything else. "I've needed to feel you like this for so long," he whispered huskily.

"I love you," she whispered.

"Hold me, Paula. Never let me go."

"Never."

"Okay, you two lovebirds. Time to break it up."

Paula gasped in embarrassment because someone had

opened the passenger door and could see what they'd been doing. While her face went scarlet, Walker broke into a wide smile that transformed him into the most handsome man she'd ever seen in her life.

"Dusty? Let me introduce you to Paula Olsen, the future Mrs. Cody in just a few hours."

"Hey— What about me?" Dusty's twin joined him.

"That one's Dex," Walker whispered in her ear. "And the one next to him is my big brother, Jesse."

She cleared her throat and sat up, eyeing each of them in turn. "To borrow a phrase from one of your oldest fans in the region, I have to say you're the best-looking set of brothers this side of the Continental Divide, not to mention the most talented men on the back of a horse I've ever seen."

Walker squeezed her hip. He couldn't seem to take his hands off her, and she didn't want him to.

Dusty whistled. "Get a look at those bluebell eyes. Are there any more at home like you?"

"No," Walker declared. "She's one of a kind." He buried his face in her silky blond hair.

"I'll say." Dex's smile had turned into a grin. "You know what, bro? You're a dark horse if I ever saw one."

"We're ecstatic for you and Walker, Paula." Jesse leaned in to kiss her cheek.

Their warmth brought her emotions to the surface. "Thank you, but I'm the one who's ecstatic. The day I met Walker at the dog parade in Markton transformed my life. Clay's, too. He loves your brother."

"Speaking of Clay, Mom and Dad are overjoyed they're going to be instant grandparents," Dusty confided. "Mom and Elly already love him. Whoever thought Walker would be the first of us to get tied down?"

"I know for a fact *Walker* didn't!" Paula's comment brought an explosion of laughter from his brothers. "To be honest I didn't think it was going to happen. He ran so hard and fast from me, I didn't know where I was half the time. It was a now-you-see-me, now-you-don't kind of thing. He drove me half-mad."

"That's our Walker," Dex said with a happy laugh.

"Until you got your arm hooked around him solid, like a good bulldogger, and brought him down for the count," Jesse said, supplying the colorful metaphor. "Looks like you got things figured out." It sounded like a private message for Walker, who grinned.

"She swept me off my feet and I didn't have a prayer," he murmured against her neck. "You guys will have to try it sometime."

They all looked so horrified, Paula burst into laughter. Walker was silently laughing, too. She felt his body shake.

"It'll happen when you least expect it," she informed them. "There I was, minding my own business when this champion rodeo hero moved in with his trick hands and his trick moves."

While Jesse chuckled, Walker levered himself from the cab. "Come here to me, darling." He reached across the console for her. "Let's make an appearance before Mom and Dad have to come looking for us. Then we've got other things to do."

"Woo-eee!" the twins cried in unison.

* * * * *

*We hope you enjoyed the first
book in the Codys' Family saga.
Watch for more stories
featuring these men and
women of the West.*

Dexter: Honorable Cowboy (July 2010)
Dusty: Wild Cowboy (August 2010)
Mark: Secret Cowboy (September 2010)
Elly: Cowgirl Bride (October 2010)
Jesse: Merry Christmas, Cowboy (November 2010)

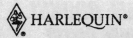

HARLEQUIN®

American ★ Romance®

COMING NEXT MONTH

Available July 13, 2010

#1313 THE LAWMAN'S LITTLE SURPRISE
Babies & Bachelors USA
Roxann Delaney

#1314 DEXTER: HONORABLE COWBOY
The Codys: The First Family of Rodeo
Marin Thomas

#1315 A MOM FOR CALLIE
Laura Bradford

#1316 FIREFIGHTER DADDY
Fatherhood
Lee McKenzie

REQUEST YOUR FREE BOOKS!
2 FREE NOVELS PLUS 2 FREE GIFTS!

HARLEQUIN®

American Romance®

Love, Home & Happiness!

YES! Please send me 2 FREE Harlequin® American Romance® novels and my 2 FREE gifts (gifts are worth about $10). After receiving them, if I don't wish to receive any more books, I can return the shipping statement marked "cancel." If I don't cancel, I will receive 4 brand-new novels every month and be billed just $4.24 per book in the U.S. or $4.99 per book in Canada. That's a saving of at least 15% off the cover price! It's quite a bargain! Shipping and handling is just 50¢ per book.* I understand that accepting the 2 free books and gifts places me under no obligation to buy anything. I can always return a shipment and cancel at any time. Even if I never buy another book from Harlequin, the two free books and gifts are mine to keep forever.

154/354 HDN E5LG

Name _____ (PLEASE PRINT) _____

Address _____ Apt. # _____

City _____ State/Prov. _____ Zip/Postal Code _____

Signature (if under 18, a parent or guardian must sign) _____

Mail to the Harlequin Reader Service:
IN U.S.A.: P.O. Box 1867, Buffalo, NY 14240-1867
IN CANADA: P.O. Box 609, Fort Erie, Ontario L2A 5X3

Not valid for current subscribers to Harlequin® American Romance® books.

Want to try two free books from another line?
Call 1-800-873-8635 or visit www.morefreebooks.com.

* Terms and prices subject to change without notice. Prices do not include applicable taxes. N.Y. residents add applicable sales tax. Canadian residents will be charged applicable provincial taxes and GST. Offer not valid in Quebec. This offer is limited to one order per household. All orders subject to approval. Credit or debit balances in a customer's account(s) may be offset by any other outstanding balance owed by or to the customer. Please allow 4 to 6 weeks for delivery. Offer available while quantities last.

Your Privacy: Harlequin is committed to protecting your privacy. Our Privacy Policy is available online at www.eHarlequin.com or upon request from the Reader Service. From time to time we make our lists of customers available to reputable third parties who may have a product or service of interest to you. If you would prefer we not share your name and address, please check here. ☐

Help us get it right—We strive for accurate, respectful and relevant communications. To clarify or modify your communication preferences, visit us at www.ReaderService.com/consumerchoice.

HAR10R

HARLEQUIN®

A Romance

FOR EVERY MOOD™

Spotlight on

Heart & Home

Heartwarming romances
where love can happen
right when you least expect it.

See the next page to enjoy a sneak peek
from Silhouette Special Edition®,
a Heart and Home series.

*Introducing McFARLANE'S PERFECT BRIDE
by USA TODAY bestselling author Christine Rimmer,
from Silhouette Special Edition®.*

Entranced. Captivated. Enchanted.

Connor sat across the table from Tori Jones and couldn't help thinking that those words exactly described what effect the small-town schoolteacher had on him. He might as well stop trying to tell himself he wasn't interested. He was powerfully drawn to her.

Clearly, he should have dated more when he was younger.

There had been a couple of other women since Jennifer had walked out on him. But he had never been entranced. Or captivated. Or enchanted.

Until now.

He wanted her—*her,* Tori Jones, in particular. Not just someone suitably attractive and well-bred, as Jennifer had been. Not just someone sophisticated, sexually exciting and discreet, which pretty much described the two women he'd dated after his marriage crashed and burned.

It came to him that he…he *liked* this woman. And that was new to him. He liked her quick wit, her wisdom and her big heart. He liked the passion in her voice when she talked about things she believed in.

He liked *her.* And suddenly it mattered all out of proportion that she might like him, too.

Was he losing it? He couldn't help but wonder. Was he cracking under the strain—of the soured economy, the McFarlane House setbacks, his divorce, the scary changes in his son? Of the changes he'd decided he needed to make in his life and himself?

Strangely, right then, on his first date with Tori Jones, he didn't care if he just might be going over the edge. He was having a great time—having *fun*, of all things—and he didn't want it to end.

Is Connor finally able to admit his feelings to Tori, and are they reciprocated?
Find out in McFARLANE'S PERFECT BRIDE
by USA TODAY bestselling author Christine Rimmer.
Available July 2010,
only from Silhouette Special Edition®.

Silhouette® *Desire*

USA TODAY bestselling author

MAUREEN CHILD

**brings you the first
of a six-book miniseries—**

Dynasties: The Jarrods

Book one:

CLAIMING HER BILLION-DOLLAR BIRTHRIGHT

Erica Prentice has set out to claim
her billion-dollar inheritance
and the man she loves.

*Available in July
wherever you buy books.*

Always Powerful, Passionate and Provocative.